THE WEIGHT OF BLOOD

THE
WEIGHT
OF BLOOD

D.B. CAREW

NEWEST PRESS
EDMONTON, AB

Library and Archives Canada Cataloguing in Publication

Title: The weight of blood / D.B. Carew.
Names: Carew, D. B., 1969- author.
Description: Series statement: A Chris Ryder thriller
Identifiers: Canadiana (print) 20200159836 | Canadiana (ebook) 20200159917 |
ISBN 9781988732923 (softcover) | ISBN 9781988732930 (EPUB)
| ISBN 9781988732947 (Kindle)
Classification: LCC PS8605.A737 W45 2020 | DDC C813/.6—dc23

NeWest Press wishes to acknowledge that the land on which we operate is Treaty 6 territory and a traditional meeting ground and home for many Indigenous Peoples, including Cree, Saulteaux, Niitsitapi (Blackfoot), Métis, and Nakota Sioux.

Board Editor: Leslie Vermeer
Cover design & typesetting: Kate Hargreaves
Cover photograph by Erol Ahmed via Unsplash
Author photograph: Matthew Carew

All Rights Reserved

NeWest Press acknowledges the Canada Council for the Arts, the Alberta Foundation for the Arts, and the Edmonton Arts Council for support of our publishing program. This project is funded in part by the Government of Canada.

201, 8540 – 109 Street
Edmonton, AB T6G 1E6
780.432.9427
www.newestpress.com

NeWest Press

No bison were harmed in the making of this book.

PRINTED AND BOUND IN CANADA
1 2 3 4 5 22 21 20

Dedicated to the memory of
Leanne Wilson and Roger Sasaki

ONE

He crept along the dark path and came to a small clearing. In the dim light, he saw what looked like blood splattered over the ground. His chest tightened. Farther ahead, he could just make out a figure lying still, face down. He approached the body cautiously, a feeling of dread intensifying with every step. He knew he should run, but instead he inched toward the body sprawled before him.

Who was it? He couldn't tell in this light, but a voice screeching inside his head told him it was someone he knew, someone he loved. He prayed that it wasn't Ann Marie. Or Stephanie. Chris slowly reached down to turn the body over. "No!"

"She's gone." Ray Owens stepped into view. He raised his Remington M24 and pointed it at Chris. "And you're next."

"No!"

"No!" Chris jolted up in bed and scrambled for the night lamp.

Beside him in bed, his girlfriend rubbed her eyes and looked at him with concern. "What's wrong, Chris?"

He didn't answer. It took him a moment to get his bearings: he was in Stephanie's Vancouver condo. His breathing was laboured, and he felt sweat trickling down his naked chest. He looked at the clock: two fifty-three in the morning. He lay back down, despairing over the fact that it was now Monday, the workday only hours away.

"It's okay. It was just a dream." Stephanie wrapped her arms around him and huddled closer. "Was it the same one?"

"Yeah," Chris whispered, upset with himself. Shivers radiated from his still-trembling body. He exhaled deeply, relieved that the danger wasn't real.

"You screamed. Want to talk about it?"

"I don't want to worry you with my problems. Sorry I woke you."

"That's all right." She touched his shoulder. "Ray can't hurt you anymore."

Chris flinched as a painful memory suddenly surfaced. He turned his head away to catch his breath.

"Another flashback?"

"Yeah," he said, waiting for his heart rate to return to normal.

"The worst is behind you now. But if you won't talk to me, promise you'll talk to Nathaniel."

"I will," he said through a heavy sigh.

"Ray tried to kill you. Nobody gets over that kind of trauma overnight."

"But that was three months ago. I'm getting tired of reliving that night. Every. Bloody. Night. And I'm tired of the nightmares. I'm tired of looking over my shoulder, expecting to see Ray coming to finish me off."

"Ray is in jail now. He can't hurt you where he is. And remember, the memories and nightmares are expected as part of your recovery. But it takes time, and it means talking these things through on a regular basis, until they're gone."

"I know. You're right. I'm seeing Nathaniel today. Hopefully it'll help."

"It will help, Chris. You're going to get through this. *We're* going to get through this ... together."

He thought back to three months earlier when Stephanie worked as a psychologist and he as a social worker at the Institute of Forensic Psychiatry. After his attack by Ray Owens, Stephanie had performed critical incident debriefing with Chris as he prepared for his return to work. She took herself off his case because of her feelings for him and insisted he see a counsellor. Eventually they started dating. Although they'd known each other for ten years, it was Chris' ordeal with Ray that brought them back into each other's lives.

"You're the best thing that's happened to me in a long time," he finally said, and kissed Stephanie.

"And I'm not going to let you forget it," she said with a smile.

"I'm serious." He paused for a moment before continuing. "When Deanna asked for a separation, all I could think about was how I'd failed as a husband, and as a father for Ann Marie. I didn't think my life could get any worse. Then Ray came along and proved me wrong. Never in a million years would I have dreamt that we'd be lying here together."

"All it took was ten years, your failed marriage, my broken engagement, and your almost getting killed."

"All I know is you're here now. I love you, and I'm not letting anything tear us apart."

TWO

Chris hadn't stepped two feet outside Stephanie's condo later that morning when the headline *Ice Cream Vendor Beaten to Death* caught his attention. He picked up the paper and skimmed the article by *Vancouver Tribune* crime reporter Lucy Chen.

> The body of a 69-year-old man was discovered Saturday by a driver on Highway 7 in Hope. The victim has been identified as Alberto Bianchi. A suspect has been taken into custody.
>
> Bianchi, an ice cream vendor, was a popular figure for generations of Hope residents, and his death has shocked his family and the local community.
>
> Bianchi's daughter, Maria Gilbert, says her father was three months away from closing down his mobile ice cream business, one he'd operated on the same route for more than 30 years.

"My father loved putting smiles on people's faces. He never hurt anyone his whole life. I just don't understand why someone would do something like this."

It's believed Bianchi was taking a back road to his home when his ice cream truck broke down. Police are asking anyone who may have noticed Bianchi or his truck to come forward.

The suspect, Marvin Aaron Goodwin, 20, was arrested at the scene. Goodwin is expected to make an appearance at the Hope courthouse today to face one count of murder.

Chris viewed an attached photo of a beaming Bianchi posing beside his ice cream truck in 1993. He sympathized with the man's family who must be struggling to come to terms with his murder.

Chris tried to kick-start his brain into work mode as he drove into the parking lot at nine in the morning. Located in Coquitlam, British Columbia, about thirty kilometres outside Vancouver, the Institute of Forensic Psychiatry provided court-ordered psychiatric assessments and treatment for people with mental health challenges who'd come into conflict with the law. Chris worked on Alpha Unit, the maximum-security remand unit. On the radio, the Boomtown Rats were singing "I Don't Like Mondays."

Chris checked in at the hospital's reception desk, manned by Horace Greening, a security officer. "Hey,

Chris, I scored a ticket for the Canucks game!" the brawny man boasted.

"Hopefully, you won't be the only one scoring. They couldn't buy a goal on Saturday." Chris couldn't resist giving the gears to Horace, a rabid fan of the Vancouver hockey team. This year, Horace wasn't alone on the bandwagon, as the Canucks had found a way to advance to the Western Conference final in the Stanley Cup playoffs. This was the first May in a number of years that players were perfecting their slapshots rather than their golf swings. "Pressure's on now. They're down two games."

"They've still got a chance," Horace said defiantly.

"A couple more games like Saturday's and they won't."

"Go, Canucks, go!" was Horace's only response.

Once in his office, Chris set down his weathered messenger bag and turned on the computer to review his email. While it warmed up, he noticed his sole remaining plant on the windowsill was in desperate need of water, with brown leaves littering the ledge. He was about to water it when a tap at his door distracted him. It was psychiatrist Marilyn Stevenson, a copy of the *Tribune* in hand. "How was your weekend?"

"Good. Yours?" Chris had been a social worker at IFP for ten years, and for most of that time, he'd worked with Marilyn, one reason he still enjoyed working there.

"A little reading and some gardening. Nice and quiet, unlike today." She handed the newspaper to Chris so he could see the headline. "Meet our new admission."

"Yeah, I read the story," he said glumly. "He's coming here today?"

"That's what Admitting tells me."

"What do we know about him?"

Dr. Stevenson shrugged. "Not a whole lot. He was found at the scene covered in ice cream and blood. So we know he likes his frozen treats," she added with a grin. Chris groaned, knowing that dark humour was a necessary coping mechanism in their line of work. "All he had on him was an expired BC medical card. Police got nowhere with him, and the staff at the pre-trial centre couldn't get anything out of him."

"He's not cooperating?"

"He doesn't appear to be deliberately withholding information. It's more a question of his mental capacity to cooperate, which is why he's been ordered here for a fitness assessment. He was triaged as a priority admission."

"How come?"

"According to the notes from pre-trial, his ability to communicate verbally is limited. It looks as if he's got severe cognitive deficits. Admitting says he's scheduled to arrive between two-thirty and three this afternoon. I plan on seeing him at three-thirty. It would be great if you could join me."

"I'll be there. I'll do a little digging before then to find out what I can about him. There's got to be family or someone who knows him."

"Keep in mind, Chris, that you're not the only one digging for information. I already had a call this morning from Lucy Chen, wanting to ask me questions about the case. I alerted Florence, who ordered me to direct all media inquiries to the communications department."

Hearing Florence's name put the usual knot in Chris' stomach. Florence Threader was the hospital's director of patient care. He knew his director was looking out for the best interests of the hospital, but his last confrontation with her had almost cost him his job. Having the Goodwin case on Florence's radar would make Chris' life more difficult than it already was.

"Thanks for the warning."

THREE

After reviewing his email, Chris walked the short distance to the Admitting office, where he found Jody sitting behind her desk. She was organizing paperwork into a large purple binder, which would become a new patient's chart.

"I hope you're having a marvellous Monday," he said with a smile. "I'm looking for the chart for Marvin Goodwin."

"Enjoy," she said, handing a file to Chris. "I'm still waiting for more information from the Crown. I'll let you know when it arrives."

"Thanks, Jody." He returned to his office and skimmed through the file, which included the assessment order from the Hope Provincial Court for a fitness assessment, the police report narrative, and the health snapshot from Surrey Pre-trial Centre. The assessment order listed a defence lawyer assigned to Marvin's case, which saved Chris from having to contact the Legal Services Society to confirm whether Marvin had a lawyer and completing a Legal Aid application if he didn't.

Next, Chris did an internet search on the Goodwin surname but couldn't find anything else on Marvin or locate any relatives. He also struck out with the ministries of Social Development and Health, as both agencies cited client privacy and demanded signed consent from Marvin before releasing anything. "Sorry I can't help you. I'm just doing my job."

"Does someone have to die before information gets shared?" Chris immediately regretted taking his frustration out on the Ministry staffer. "Hey, I apologize. I totally get the need to protect personal information. It's just that I've seen too many situations where withholding information has worked against the very client it was designed to protect." He had also fielded far too many calls from distraught family members left with unanswered questions as to why the information they needed was unavailable.

"Apology accepted. I get a lot of complaints about our privacy procedures."

He decided to focus his energy on finding creative ways to obtain the information he was looking for.

He called a probation officer he knew at Adult Community Corrections. After a few rings, Mason

Jean picked up, and the two men engaged in idle chit-chat before Chris got down to business. "I'm trying to see if one of my patients has a file with you guys."

He was met with silence, then, "This wouldn't have anything to do with Ray Owens, would it?"

Hearing Ray's name was like a kick to the stomach. It took Chris a moment to recover. "No, it's not about him. It's a guy named Marvin Goodwin. You probably heard the story on the news, the so-called Ice Cream Killer?"

"Yeah, I know the one. Gimme a second, I'll see what I've got." Chris heard the sound of fingers hitting a keyboard. "Nope, he's clean. At least, he was up until now."

"Thanks. That helps."

"No problem. When are you gonna buy me that beer you owe me?"

"Name the time and place, and I'll be there. Cheers."

Chris' next call was to Sergeant Brandon Ryan, a member of the Major Crimes Unit of the RCMP. They'd met three months earlier when Chris had been shot and had since become friends. He explained why he was calling and asked for information about Marvin Goodwin.

Brandon put Chris on hold while he did a background search on the accused. "Nope, no other files on record."

"It was worth a try. Thanks."

"Any time. From what I've heard, that case is freaking bizarre. It's no wonder he's at your place."

"Why do you say that?"

"For starters, the kid was discovered at the scene covered in blood, but no one knows how he got himself out into the middle of nowhere. It's a long walk from the nearest residential area, and he doesn't look like the walking kind."

"I read the police report. Mr. Bianchi was attacked with a tire iron?"

"Yeah, looks like his truck broke down and he was fixing a flat tire. Blood everywhere. The kid wouldn't say a word to the arresting officers other than 'home.' Good luck is all I can say."

"It's looking like we'll need it."

"Oh, and while I've got you on the line, I received an invitation from Elizabeth. She's holding a ceremony at Woodland Park to dedicate a bench to her father. You get one?"

Chris' head started to throb. It was Chris who had discovered John Carrier's body in Woodland Park, and it was Chris who had rescued Elizabeth Carrier from her abductors in that same park. Woodland Park was also where Ray Owens had shot him. "Yeah, I got one."

"I thought maybe we could go together and —"

"Uh ... I don't know. I haven't decided whether I'm going."

"Oh, okay. You have other plans?"

"It's not that." Chris took a deep breath. "That park brings up a whole load of stuff for me, you know. I'm not sure I'm ready to go back yet. As much as I'd like to be there for Elizabeth ... I just don't know."

"Hey, no worries. If you show, great. Otherwise, I'll pass on your regards, okay?"

"Yeah. Sorry, Brandon."

Chris hung up, then lowered his head and massaged his aching temples. He suddenly felt a lot older than his thirty-eight-year-old athletic build would suggest. *Will I ever be able to think about Woodland Park without the urge to puke? Or keep Ray out of my head without the urge to strangle him?*

His thoughts drifted back to three months earlier when he'd found Ray's cellphone and discovered John Carrier's body. Ray had almost destroyed Chris' life. Following what the media referred to as the Murder at Woodland Park, Ray had conned his way into being admitted to the Institute of Forensic Psychiatry, where he proceeded to do what he did best: terrorize those around him. The assessment hadn't found any evidence to suggest that Ray suffered from acute mental illness. On the contrary, Dr. Stevenson's report found that he was in full control of his mental faculties and knew precisely what he was doing when he committed his criminal acts. He did, however, exhibit the classic symptoms of antisocial personality disorder and psychopathic traits. Ray was considered a high risk to reoffend, and there was no evidence to suggest that he would benefit from rehabilitation.

Even though Ray was in custody awaiting trial on a number of charges, Chris still felt a paralyzing fear whenever he thought of him and the threats he'd made against his family. Chris' fear that Ray would hurt Stephanie was made worse by the fact that she now worked as a psychologist in the very facility where Ray was detained.

Chris had good days and bad days when it came to keeping Ray out of his head. This was turning out to be a bad one.

FOUR

Chris made his way to Alpha Unit to meet Dr. Stevenson. He would assist her in assessing Marvin's fitness to stand trial: whether Marvin could understand the basics of the court process as well as his ability to communicate with his lawyer.

Chris was hoping today's meeting would give him a phone number for a family member so he could find out background information about Marvin and what he had been doing in the days leading up to his arrest. That would help Marilyn with her report on Marvin for his next court date.

Before his confrontation with Ray Owens, Chris had ventured onto Alpha Unit countless times without incident. Today, however, his body tensed, just as it had on every occasion since his clash with Ray. He waited for the anxiety to pass.

Bracing himself, he unlocked the door of the unit and walked inside.

Alpha Unit could accommodate twenty-two patients and had been designed with safety and cost effectiveness, not aesthetic purposes, in mind. Patients' rooms consisted mainly of a bed, drawer set, and small writing table. Washrooms were shared. In the three common rooms, patients could watch TV, listen to music, and socialize. A locked door separated this area from the rest of the unit. On the other side of the unit, a large dining room was located next to the nursing station, where dietary staff delivered meals on large food trolleys. One could be forgiven for confusing the Alpha and Beta units as they looked like mirror images of each other, with off-white walls, blue flooring, and the same institutional equipment. Even the interview rooms were replicas of each other.

Alpha was buzzing with activity, something Chris likened to organized chaos, as nurses prepared one of Chris' patients to be discharged and transported back to Surrey Pre-trial, while another patient was due to be admitted to that departing patient's bed. Chris made his way to the nursing station. This room held patients' charts and medications and had large windows to optimize viewing patient activity. He was greeted by head nurse Alex Dunbar, who, at six foot two and two hundred twenty pounds, commanded attention wherever he went. The two men engaged in small talk until Dr. Stevenson joined them. Alex introduced them to Corinne, a second-year nursing student starting a preceptorship at the hospital, and explained that he'd suggested she sit in on the meeting, after receiving Marvin's nod of approval. The four headed to an interview room to discuss Marvin.

"How's Mr. Goodwin doing?" Marilyn asked.

"Keeping to himself," Alex replied. "I gave him an orientation to the unit about half an hour ago, showed him his room, the usual routine. I also did the intake assessment interview—or I should say, I attempted to."

"What do you mean?" Chris asked.

"He couldn't answer many of the questions; he'd just repeat the last word or two of what I asked him. We've kept a close eye on him to make sure no one gives him a hard time."

Dr. Stevenson looked at Chris. "Any luck with family?"

He shook his head. "Nothing yet. I also spoke with probation and the RCMP, and neither has anything on him."

With the preliminaries out of the way, Alex left the room to get Marvin, returning a few minutes later with the young man by his side. The differences between the two men were striking. Against Alex's large frame, Marvin appeared even shorter and thinner than he actually was, his hospital-issued blue sweats hanging loosely. His pale complexion contrasted starkly with the nurse's healthy colouring, and his long, unkempt brown hair looked like it hadn't been washed in days. Marvin looked around the room nervously, then kept his eyes downcast.

Chris offered him a chair, and Marvin cautiously sat down.

After introducing the team, Dr. Stevenson started the interview.

"How are things going for you on the unit, Mr. Goodwin? Would you prefer Mr. Goodwin or Marvin?" No reply to either question. She continued.

"Do you know why you've been admitted here?" Marvin offered no response other than a slight unintelligible mumbling under his breath.

Chris suspected the young man was feeling intimidated by all the questions from strangers. An idea popped into his head. He pulled out a pen, its hard plastic casing removed so it couldn't be used as a weapon, and handed it to the young man. "Marvin ... is it okay if I call you Marvin?"

"Marvin," was the sole response.

Chris handed him a blank piece of paper. "Maybe you can write down anything you'd like us to know about you, okay?"

"Okay," the young man repeated mechanically. He scribbled something on the paper, then sat quietly with his hands folded.

"Can I take a look?" Chris asked.

Without any expression or eye contact, Marvin

handed over the paper. On it, neatly printed, was the word *home*.

"That's great, Marvin. Where is home?"

"Home."

"Can you write down your phone number?"

"Phone number." To everyone's surprise, Marvin wrote down a local telephone number.

"Do you live alone in your home, Marvin?"

"Home." He gently put the pen down on the table and stared at it. Chris took this to mean that he was done for the day.

"Is it okay if I take the sheet with your phone number?"

"Phone number." The young man handed the paper to Chris without making eye contact. He then stood up to leave, and Alex escorted him back to his room.

"Well, it's a start," Dr. Stevenson remarked. "A slow one, but a start nonetheless. At first glance, he doesn't look fit to stand trial."

"It's hard to picture him carrying out that crime," Chris said.

The psychiatrist nodded. "But that's for the police to sort out."

Alex returned to the interview room. "So, what do you think we're dealing with here? He's obviously got some kind of cognitive problem."

"I'd say Marvin's got a moderate degree of intellectual disorder. I also think he falls along the extreme end of autism spectrum disorder." She turned to Corinne, the nursing student. "ASD would explain Marvin's problems with social interactions and his communication challenges. Did you notice how he repeated the last few words of the questions he was asked?" Corinne nodded.

"That's called echolalia. Repetitive behaviours and in some cases cognitive delays are also present with ASD. I'm going to have my work cut out for me with Marvin's assessment, but I'll also ask Psychology to see him," Dr. Stevenson continued. "Hopefully, he'll agree to some basic testing. It would also be very helpful to have background information from his family, Chris. Maybe the number he wrote down will help. Someone must be looking for him."

"I'll see what I can do."

"By the way, nice touch with the pen. He seemed to respond to your approach."

"Thanks. I'm interested in finding out where this phone number leads me."

FIVE

Chris dialled the number Marvin had written. After several rings with no response, he hung up. He was about to dial again when his phone rang.

"You calling me?" a male voice on the other end demanded.

"Uh, I was looking for a family member ... for Marvin."

"Goodwin?"

"Yes. Are you a relative?"

Brief silence. "Who are you?" the man demanded again.

"I'm a social worker at the Institute of Forensic Psychiatry. Marvin's been admitted for a psychiatric assessment. He gave me this number. Are you his father? His brother?"

"Yeah. Michael, his brother."

"I'm sorry to be talking with you under these circumstances. Unfortunately, your brother has been charged with a very serious offence."

"It's a bullshit charge. There's no way Marv would've done what they say he did."

"So you're aware of the charge?"

"Hell, yeah. It's been all over the news. But that doesn't mean it's true. He wouldn't hurt a fly."

"That's why I'm calling, to find out what I can about your brother. Marvin hasn't been able to give us much information."

"I can tell you he didn't kill anyone."

"Okay, Michael, but that's part of a police investigation and I'm not involved with that. Our job is to see if your brother is fit to stand trial."

"You don't understand. Marv shouldn't have been charged in the first place. It ain't fair. His whole life, people have called him stupid and retarded. Now they're calling him a killer. You gotta help him!" The man shouted into the phone.

"All right, I hear you." *Time to change tactics.* "Look, Michael, I want to help your brother. But to do that, I need to know more about him. For example, does he have a family doctor?"

There was a long pause. "Marv hasn't seen a doctor in years."

"Okay, do you remember the name of the doctor who last saw him?"

"Yeah, it was some guy named Bond, like in those movies."

"Do you remember how long ago that might have been?"

"Marv was a kid, that's all I remember."

"Does Marvin have a team working with him, like a psychiatrist or home care?"

Another long pause. "I gotta go. Listen, tell them Marv is innocent. You gotta do that for him. He doesn't deserve to go to jail; he'd die in there. Have you seen him? Have you actually met him yet?"

"Yes, I was with him just a few minutes ago. He's settling in well with the unit."

"No one is hassling him, right? He doesn't deserve shit from no one."

"Marvin's okay. He's on a unit where there are staff to help him."

"And he gave you my number? Go figure, he must have liked you or something. Oh yeah, make sure he gets the *Tribune* every day. He reads the sports section, especially about the Canucks. He has a thing for reading player stats. As long as he has a paper, he'll be fine. And paper to colour, he likes to colour. Take good care of him, okay?" The line went dead.

Chris sat perplexed about the conversation he'd just had, a conversation that left him with more questions than answers. At least now, though, he had somewhere to start: Dr. Bond. He Googled medical offices with physicians on staff named Bond, which narrowed his search to three clinics in the Vancouver area.

He called the offices and his efforts paid off. The second medical clinic confirmed having Marvin's childhood medical records archived, and the receptionist agreed to fax them to the number Chris provided.

Pleased that he'd accomplished something, he prepared to leave work for the day, but first, he called Alpha Unit to pass on the information about Marvin liking the *Tribune*. Still, he couldn't shake the feeling that he'd only scratched the surface of the Goodwin case.

SIX

On his drive from work that afternoon, Chris' thoughts
turned to his upcoming session with Nathaniel Power.
When Stephanie stopped her counselling role with
Chris, she recommended he seek additional therapy
through his hospital's Employee Assistance Program.
And now that they were dating, she'd made it clear
that she couldn't continue with their relationship if
he wasn't willing to work on his recovery from PTSD.
Chris reluctantly agreed to therapy because he was
willing to do just about anything to continue seeing
Stephanie. He'd started working with a new psychologist and they'd seen each other twice. Nathaniel used
a cognitive therapy approach to counselling, with the
goal of helping Chris understand and change the way
he thought about his trauma and its effects on him.

Before entering Nathaniel's building, Chris checked his phone and read a new text from Stephanie. "Good luck with your session." The love emoji brought a smile to his face as he entered the office.

"So Chris, in our last session, we identified Post Traumatic Stress Disorder symptoms related to what happened to you at Woodland Park. These include the recurring and intrusive images and flashbacks you've had associated with discovering James Carrier's body, as well as disturbing thoughts and feelings related to the trauma of being shot by Ray Owens. Correct?"

Chris nodded.

"You noted another symptom involves sleep, difficulty falling or staying asleep, as well as nightmares. Yes?"

"Yeah, and anxiety. I get panic attacks."

"Have you had difficulties with concentration or irritability?"

Chris briefed him on his recent outburst over the telephone with the staffer. "That's definitely not something I would normally do. But my concentration isn't that bad. Work actually helps as a distraction from ... from all this other stuff."

"By stuff, you're referring to your anxiety, sleep problems, and flashbacks?"

"Yeah, it's pretty stressful." Chris exhaled loudly. "I used to deal with it by running. Going for a run on a trail used to melt away my stress. And listening to music used to help by distracting me from whatever was bugging me. But now ... I can be listening to music or running and all of a sudden I realize I've been thinking about Ray Owens for the last twenty minutes."

"Give me an example of what you'd be thinking about with Ray Owens."

"Wondering what's he's scheming and planning to do next, to hurt me and my family. Or my mind will go back to that day at Woodland Park when he held the rifle on me. The thoughts just creep into my head, it's hard for me to catch them, you know, to stop from thinking about them, and it's *so* mentally draining to get them out of my head."

"Well, exercise and listening to music are positive strategies. We can build on those by adding deep-breathing exercises. So, for example, when you find yourself getting anxious, slowing down your breathing can help, as well as learning to relax the muscles in your body when you become tense, and focussing your attention on inhaling and exhaling. Another strategy would be using grounding techniques. Grounding can be particularly helpful when you experience a flashback because touching something around you and describing it in detail can help return your focus to the present. I've got some handouts on this if you're interested."

"Sure, it's worth a try."

Nathaniel stood up, went to his filing cabinet, and retrieved a booklet, which he handed to Chris. "You mentioned your work earlier." Chris leaned back into his chair. "Do you like your job?"

"Wow, that's a loaded question," Chris replied with a nervous laugh.

"How so?"

Chris took a moment to collect his thoughts. "I enjoy working with patients and their families. For many families, this is their first experience with having a family member with mental health issues or being involved with the forensic system. I appreciate being able to provide information about the hospital, and I spend a fair amount of time listening to family members tell their story of how the illness and the crime has impacted them. I never lose sight of the fact that the patient I'm working with is someone's father, son, husband, or brother. In some instances, we help reconnect patients with their families after a period of being estranged from each other, and that's extremely rewarding."

"Do you think your decision to work in a helping profession, and your interest in helping families, has been influenced by your own family experience, with your mother dying when you were young?"

Chris winced involuntarily.

"I can see it's a sensitive subject."

"I'm sure you could make a connection between the impact my mother's murder had on me as a kid and the fact that I relate to families when they're going through a rough time."

"The question is, do you agree with that connection?"

"Yeah. I do, especially around the feeling of being powerless. There was nothing I could do to save my mother and that really bothered me growing up. So I guess you could say I empathize when a patient's family member reaches out for help. I do everything I can to help."

"I imagine that can be stressful, too, putting a lot of responsibility on yourself. That, and the fact that you work with vulnerable individuals, many coming from difficult backgrounds, admitted under difficult circumstances, and often charged with serious crimes."

"It can be," Chris said in a subdued voice.

"What do you see as the greatest challenges for you?"

"Well, there's the fallout from the crime, as you pointed out, working with a patient without judging him for the crime he's charged with committing. It's also difficult when a patient is discharged from hospital and for whatever reason doesn't connect with services in his community."

"Are you referring to mental health after-care services?"

"Yeah, and homelessness. Many patients end up on the street because they can't afford or find available housing. Not to mention the problems with addiction, and now with the fentanyl crisis, I often worry that someone I worked with will overdose. Then there are my patients who cycle through the hospital on a regular basis. They get discharged when they're stable. But either they don't have adequate services in the community or they don't follow through with appointments and medication, so they get sick again. They commit another crime, get charged and incarcerated, and are admitted back with us. The cycle continues."

"The criminalization of the mentally ill," Nathaniel said.

"Yeah, it takes its toll." Chris massaged his temples to ward off a looming headache.

"I can see the impact it has on you, just from watching you talk about it," Nathaniel said.

"You're not the only one. Deanna wanted me to leave my job and look for something less stressful when we were married but ..." Chris' voice trailed off.

"Do you think your job had a negative impact on your marriage?"

"It didn't help," Chris quipped. "But no, I have to own my part with that." He thought back to Deanna's parting words. *Chris, I think it would be best if Ann Marie and I moved out for a while.* The words stung him as intensely now as they had nine months ago. In the end, it was Chris who moved out.

"How do you feel about that now?"

Chris paused briefly, subconsciously fidgeting with his left finger, as if twirling a phantom wedding ring. "The warning signs were there, but I didn't see them, or didn't want to see them. I remember Deanna saying I was spending too much time at work, that I was bringing it home with me, both literally and figuratively. She also said she felt distant from me, that we weren't connecting in any meaningful way. It's crazy when I look back on that now, but there was a part of me back then that actually thought it was more Deanna's problem than mine. I thought she was looking too hard to find a problem."

"What do you think the problem was?"

"Oh boy, where do I start?" Chris said glumly. "I guess if I'm being brutally honest, part of the problem goes back to what I was saying earlier about my mother's murder. It's taken a long time for me to realize that there's a part of me that's afraid to commit fully in a relationship out of fear that I'll lose them."

"The way you lost your mother?" Nathaniel said.

"Yeah."

"That's pretty insightful."

"Better late than never, I suppose."

"How are things between you and Deanna now?"

"We're okay. After our separation, I made a commitment to be the best father possible to Ann Marie. As part of the agreement, we decided that Ann Marie would live with her mother, and I see her on Tuesdays and most Saturdays. It works out pretty well."

"And you're seeing someone now, Stephanie, is it?"

Chris nodded. "Yeah. We've actually known each other about ten years. When I first discovered I had feelings for Stephanie, she was seeing someone and ended up getting engaged. We kinda went our separate ways for a while after that. Her engagement broke off and by the time we reconnected a few years later, Deanna and I were married."

"How are things between you two now?"

"Good. But sometimes I feel guilty, like maybe I don't deserve to be happy. Pretty messed up, I know."

"I wouldn't say that. Relationships are complicated and require constant work by both partners to be successful. But I believe everyone deserves to be happy."

Chris stayed silent.

"Speaking of relationships," Nathaniel continued, "I'd like to touch back on Ray Owens."

Just hearing Ray's name made Chris feel sick to his stomach. "What do you want to know about Ray?"

"Well, you've said previously he was admitted at your hospital on two occasions, correct?"

"Yeah. And both times, he was considered fit to stand trial and responsible for his charges, meaning he knew full well what he was doing when he committed his crimes. In fact, the second time, after what happened at Woodland Park, he actually got himself admitted at IFP just to be a shit disturber and harass me." Chris saw Nathaniel's look of surprise. "I'm not kidding. He told me as much himself. He faked hearing voices and thought he was too smart for the psychiatrist, but she saw right through him. We all did."

"So what was the outcome of that admission?"

"Dr. Stevenson did the assessment and also asked Psychology to see him for psychopathy testing. We don't normally request this type of testing because there isn't a strong link between psychopathy and a severe and persistent mental illness. But she wanted to do one with Ray for the very fact that he didn't exhibit symptoms of mental illness. Anyway, the testing confirmed what was suspected, that he had significant psychopathic traits."

"Such as?"

"Well, for starters, Ray tested high for superficial charm and glibness as well as pathological lying. He was callous and highly manipulative—he lacks empathy. He exhibited poor behavioural control and refused to accept responsibility for his actions. He showed no remorse for the pain he caused others." Chris took a deep breath. "He makes me so mad, especially when he attempts to make a mockery of the mental health and forensic system by trying to fake that he has a mental illness. He gives a bad name to those who struggle with genuine symptoms of mental illness, for those who do respond to medication and other forms of treatment."

"So Ray is currently in custody waiting for his next court date?"

"Yep."

"In your whole description of Ray, you left out what I would consider one of the most important aspects, that he's your brother."

"Half-brother. I'm not in denial, if that's what you're wondering. But it's also something that obviously I'm not proud of, so I don't make a point of announcing it to everyone."

"Are you ashamed of your biological connection?"

"Yeah. I despise everything he stands for. But there's nothing I can do about it, and he knows it, and he reminds me of it every chance he gets." Chris felt his anxiety rising. He looked through the booklet Nathaniel had given him and tried a breathing exercise, counting back from ten to one. The anxiety slowly began to subside.

"That's very good, Chris. I'm impressed."

"Thanks. I'll check these exercises out."

"Please do, and let me know what you think."

Nathaniel looked at the clock on his wall. "I'd suggest we stop here for today. How does that sound?"

"Sure," Chris said. He suddenly felt mentally drained.

Nathaniel seemed to pick up on this feeling. "We covered a lot of ground this afternoon. It would be natural to feel tired, overwhelmed even. But it won't last."

Chris got up and headed for the door. "Hope so. I look forward to the day when Ray is a distant memory."

As he exited the building, Chris texted Stephanie, "Survived it," and added a smiley face emoji.

SEVEN

Chris headed to his apartment in Burnaby, located about fifteen kilometres from Stephanie's condo. Stephanie was hosting a dinner for her mother, so Chris resigned himself to being alone for the evening. He'd left it up to her to decide when the time was right to introduce him to each of her divorced parents, and evidently tonight was not the night.

He had his own share of family drama. An argument with his father three months earlier had ended with Chris declaring that the next time he would see the old man would be at his funeral. So it was a pretty safe bet that he wouldn't be introducing Stephanie to his father any time soon, let alone inviting him over for supper.

On the other hand, he would have given the world for a chance to introduce Stephanie to his mother. In his heart, he knew his mother and Stephanie would have liked each other.

He surveyed his sparsely decorated living room and was reminded that Stephanie's entry into his life brought with it hope for a new beginning. He smiled as he recalled her suggestions for livening up the apartment, starting by adding colour to contrast the boring eggshell walls and equally unimaginative beige carpet. Lately, she'd also hinted at larger plans, plans involving them getting a place of their own. She'd shared her vision for their future and wanted to hear his. But Chris' vision for the future was clouded by uncertainty. He wasn't sure if it was fear of commitment or something else that held him back, but it was uncertainty that kept him up at night.

A phone call interrupted his gloomy thoughts. "Daddy! What are we doing tomorrow?"

"Hi, Sweetie!" Hearing the excitement in his daughter's voice instantly elevated Chris' mood. "I was thinking that we could pick out a movie to watch back here, and *maybe* we could go to the Vancouver Aquarium with Stephanie on Saturday. Would you like that?"

"Yes! Can we go to Wilbur's, too?"

Chris thought for a moment. Wilbur's restaurant had been a date-night destination for him and Deanna before Ann Marie was born, and afterwards it had become part of their weekend tradition as a family. It somehow felt wrong to take Stephanie there with his daughter, at least at this point, so he opted for an alternative. "How about the White Spot on the way to the aquarium? They've got great milkshakes."

"Yay! I can't wait!" his daughter squealed. "Mommy wants to talk to you now. Love you, Daddy." She was gone before Chris had a chance to say *I love you* back, and he could hear her sharing the news of their outing with her mother.

Deanna came on the line. "So you're taking our little angel to the aquarium on the weekend."

"Yeah, and I ... was thinking Stephanie would join us, if that's okay with you."

After what Chris felt was an endless pause, Deanna responded. "Yeah ... yeah, it's okay. Walter has joined us many times. Uh, I don't mean *many* times, but the three of us have gone to movies and the beach together. Uh, gosh, this is bit awkward, isn't it?"

"I'm sorry, Dee. I can come up with something else."

"No, no. It's fine. When will you be picking Ann Marie up tomorrow?"

"Is six o'clock okay?"

"Sounds great. We'll see you then."

"Thanks, Dee." After he hung up, it struck him that Deanna had sounded a little subdued, and he wondered whether he'd caught her off guard about Stephanie. Still, ever since he'd brought their relationship out into the open with Deanna, he'd felt a huge weight lift off his shoulder.

He reached for his iPod and soon the Tragically Hip was resounding through his apartment.

EIGHT

Chris awoke the next morning feeling poorly rested and out of sorts. His sleep had been disturbed by another bad dream, but he considered himself lucky because he couldn't remember what this one had been about, unlike the usual nightmares full of rotting corpses that were imprinted into his memory. He figured these nightmares, all stemming from his ordeal in Woodland Park, would likely be a focus in his sessions with Nathaniel.

Opening his door to grab the morning paper, he did a double take when he read the headline *Exclusive: Interview with Ray Owens.* He knew the *Tribune's* Lucy Chen was working on a series of stories about the murders at Woodland Park. She'd approached him several times for an interview about his discovery of the body of James Carrier as well as his rescue of Carrier's daughter, Elizabeth. What she was really after, Chris figured, was some juicy tidbits on his fateful encounters with Ray.

Ordered by his director not to talk to anyone in the media, however, he had turned down all of Lucy's requests. That hadn't stopped her from running an earlier story featuring him under the headline *Reluctant Hero of Woodland Park*. She'd done her research, he had to admit, and had managed to dig up information about the murder of his mother when he was a young boy.

Now, still reeling from the fallout of that story, including the unhappy memories it had stirred up, he was staring in disbelief at Ray's name on the front page. As repulsed as Chris was with the idea, he couldn't resist reading the article.

Lucy prefaced the piece by outlining her repeated attempts to get permission to interview Ray. Administration officials at the West Coast Correctional Centre had finally agreed to permit the interview, provided she adhered to their strict guidelines, including their insistence that she follow a pre-approved list of topics covered in a question-and-answer format.

The article opened with a description of the interview room at the correctional centre, then described Ray as "malodorous, with yellow-stained teeth, greasy-looking skin, and unkempt thinning grey hair." He wore an orange correctional jumpsuit, and he was supervised by two burly male guards.

LC: Mr. Owens, your current charges include two counts of murder in connection with the deaths of James Carrier and Dale Goode. You've also been charged with the attempted murder of Chris Ryder. Have you —

RO: Actually, Lucy, you've got that wrong. The Ryder charge is completely bogus. There was no attempt at murdering him. What happened there was nothing more than simple assault. And as far as the other charges go, I intend to show that I can't be held responsible for what allegedly happened. I wasn't in my right mind. But I'm not gonna talk any more about that 'cause this is still before the court, and I have nothing but respect for the court, even though they have a clear bias against me.

LC: Why did you agree to be interviewed?

RO: I'm glad you asked that, Lucy. Unlike Chris Ryder, who thinks he's too good to talk to common folk like you and me, I believe in giving the people what they want. Let's face it, you do, too, which is why you're here. People want to hear what I have to say 'cause they know I'm gonna give it to them straight up.

LC: What kind of message do you want to convey?

RO: That I'm not the monster I've been made out to be.

LC: Can you elaborate on what you mean?

RO: I'd love to. I know it's popular right now to think that I'm a bad person and I've "allegedly" done bad things. But I'm not bad at all. I'm just a guy who happens to hear voices telling me to do bad things. I reached out for help but it was never there for me.

LC: Are you suggesting you're a victim?

RO: Exactly! I'm a victim! I read an article the other day in your fine paper about the dismal state of social services for young children in care. When I reflect on my life, I realize I too am the victim of a broken social services system. I was taken as a young, defenceless child and thrown to the wolves. Dumped in foster homes where I was abused and victimized, time and time again. Did I give up? Hell, no! I picked myself up and got on with life. Now I hear these terrible voices that tell me to do horrible things. Have I given up? Hell, no! I'm a survivor.

LC: There are people who think you're a dangerous man. Some experts have gone so far as to say that you should remain in prison for the maximum amount of time. How would you respond to these statements?

RO: Like the so-called experts who put me in foster care to be abused and victimized? Let me tell you something. There are kids today being beaten and bullied at the hands of foster families and incompetent government officials that have no business being near children. Those kids today are going to be tomorrow's criminals if nothing's done to fix that broken system. Are those the "experts" you're talking about? And what about the "experts" at IFP who say I don't hear voices. What do they know? Look how I've been treated my whole life. They're the ones who should be on trial, not me. Experts? What a joke!

LC: We're down to our final question. What would you say to your victims and their families if they were here right now?

RO: I'm disappointed in you, Lucy, 'cause you twist things around so I come across looking like the bad guy. Listen, I've had some crappy things happen to me, but I've dealt with 'em and always landed on my feet. But since you're so interested in families, maybe you should ask my brother, Ryder, how he feels.

LC: Ryder? Chris Ryder? Are you saying Chris Ryder is your brother?

RO: That's right!

LC: How?

RO: Ha! Your investigative journalist skills aren't as sharp as you thought, are they? I'm willing to bet there's a lot you don't know about Ryder.

LC: What can you tell me about you and Chris Ryder being brothers?

RO: Well, I can tell you my father knocked up some woman who turned out to be Ryder's mother. For some reason, my old man stuck with Ryder's mother and ditched me, even though I was born first! The way I see it, Ryder's the one who should have been abandoned, not me.

LC: Did you ever meet your mother?

RO: Never got the pleasure. I got thrown to the wolves of the Ministry while Ryder got a silver spoon.

LC: How long have you and Mr. Ryder known this?

RO: Our time is up for today, Lucy. You'll have to ask my dear brother that yourself. And if you're talking to him, tell him I said hi.

Chris stared blankly into space, dumbfounded at what he'd just read. The *Tribune* slipped out of his hands and fell to the floor in a mess of scattered sheets.

His shock eventually gave way to anger. He was angry with Lucy for interviewing Ray and giving him an audience to fulfill his narcissistic need for attention. He was angry with Ray for using every opportunity he could to harass him, while completely dismissing the pain and torment he had inflicted on so many people. But Chris was mostly angry for allowing himself to be manipulated by Ray's games. He hated Ray, hated that they were half-brothers, and especially hated that now the whole world would know they were related.

When Ray first boasted three months earlier that they shared the same father, Chris had hoped against hope that it was nothing more than a taunt. But his father confirmed the fact, as well as the fact that Ray had been placed in Ministry care. Chris had then done research on Ray's time with the Children's Ministry. He knew that Ray had gone on to wreak havoc on his foster sister and foster mother, leading to his removal from the home and the start of a very long record of juvenile and adult criminal offences.

But Chris also knew that he himself had fared only marginally better as a child. His father had also become indifferent towards him after his mother was murdered, and it was sheer luck that Chris had a maternal aunt who stepped forward to raise him from a young age. He had grown up with many unanswered questions about his mother and the circumstances surrounding her murder. Now he was left with one more question. Had his mother known about Ray?

But his biggest fear, now that he knew about his and Ray's biological connection, was that he might share unhealthy personality traits with his half-brother. *Was he really that different from him?*

NINE

Chris arrived at his office to find a scribbled note from David Evans, his manager, attached to his computer monitor, informing him that an emergency meeting had been called for nine o'clock that morning. He scrambled to the conference room and grabbed one of the last remaining chairs. Scanning the room, he noticed that the assembled group included psychiatrists, nurses, social workers, psychologists, and family practitioners. None of his co-workers knew what the meeting was about, and the suspense hit its peak when Florence Threader, their director, made her entrance. At five feet eight inches tall and broomstick thin, she cut an imposing figure. The room fell silent.

"Thank you for making yourselves available on short notice," Florence said, taking over the meeting.

Chris watched her scan the room, getting the distinct impression that she was searching for someone. And when her eyes met his, he had the uneasy feeling that this someone was him. He looked away.

"I wish I could say good morning to you all, but the fact of the matter is this isn't a good morning." She held a newspaper in her hand. "I trust you've all seen the story in today's *Tribune*?" Heads nodded and bodies shifted uncomfortably in their seats. Florence continued. "The popular perception is that we're releasing mentally disordered offenders into the community without considering the needs of their victims or accounting for the risks our patients may pose to the general public. While we know that's not the case, recent events haven't helped shake that fear."

To emphasize her point, she held up a copy of the *Tribune* from the previous week with the headline *Patient Missing from IFP*. "As you know, Perry Matthews was reported missing when he failed to return on time from a day leave. He returned an hour later with the explanation that he'd missed his bus connection. But in that hour, all hell broke loose."

Chris recalled the situation clearly. Florence was referring to the fact that part of the protocol for dealing with unauthorized absences involved IFP staff informing the local RCMP detachment of a missing person. In Perry's case, the RCMP broadcast his absence on their Twitter feed along with an unflattering photo of the man; a short while later, the *Tribune* was reporting the incident on its website. Florence was livid.

"There's not a week goes by without IFP being in the news for one reason or another," she went on in a strained voice. "And now with a provincial election on the horizon, it's become standard procedure for politicians of every stripe to proclaim their 'tough on crime' stance, with our patients paying the price for getting lumped into that category. I had an unpleasant call this morning from the Minister of Health about this particular incident, asking questions about our process for allowing patients access to the community. As you all know, we rely on the Ministry of Health for funding, so upsetting the Minister generally doesn't help our cause."

She sighed and pointed to that morning's *Tribune*. "Today's article on Ray Owens will only add fuel to the fire, and no doubt there'll be a firestorm of misconceptions that all of our patients are dangerous like him."

She loosened her grip on the paper and placed it on the table. "That being said, we can't be blind to public perception, and we can't lose their confidence in the work we do. As a result, I've ordered a review of our community access process. And until that review has been completed, I'm placing patient leaves on hold. The only exception will be patients attending community programs with our staff. I know this is going to affect a lot of people you're working with, and you'll be fielding concerned calls from patients and their families. I've asked David to lend support to you in that regard. And our communications department has prepared an FAQ for easy reference. Don't think of it as a script, but more of a guideline that I want you to follow. Any questions?"

No one spoke up. Everyone was either too surprised or too intimidated to question the director.

"No? Good. Have a nice day."

Chris did have questions he wanted to ask. Instead of cancelling day leaves, why not hold a press conference to explain the robust process for determining a patient's access to the community, including the fact that community access privileges were granted on a gradual basis and only after careful consideration? Why not take a proactive approach and provide public education about mental illness and the forensic system? Why not talk about the positive stories of patients who'd made a successful move from hospital to community?

He was debating the merits of raising these questions when Florence approached him. "Can I speak with you for a minute?" He knew he had no choice in the matter.

"I understand you're working with Dr. Stevenson on the Marvin Goodwin case."

Chris nodded. He was about to say something but Florence beat him to it. "There's a prime example of what I was talking about. There's a lot of anger right now toward that young man, someone we at IFP see as obviously mentally compromised. The media are all over this case. The *Tribune* tried to get information from Marilyn, and she wisely informed me about it. Have they tried speaking with you?"

"No. I—"

"Do not speak with anyone. It's not my style to micromanage, so I won't do that here. I actually wanted Gerald assigned to this case, but David suggested otherwise. As long as you're working it, don't speak with the media. Don't talk to *anyone* about this case. And that goes especially for Lucy Chen. I don't want you talking with her about Ray Owens either. Is that understood?"

"I understand."

"Good. I'm anticipating the assessment of Mr. Goodwin will be done soon and he can be discharged from IFP back to Surrey Pre-trial without any complications." She paused and gave Chris a perturbed look. "Why is it that I continue to learn more and more about you and your personal life through the *Tribune*? Your family connection to Ray, for instance. Why didn't you disclose that with me when he was admitted here?"

"I only found out recently myself and ... uh ... I am still coming to terms with it."

"Are there any more revelations you are 'still coming to terms with' that I should be aware of?"

Chris shook his head.

"Good. We can do without any more distractions, can't we?" With that, she marched out of the room.

Watching his director file away reminded Chris of a tornado, touching down and causing chaos before storming off in another direction to lay waste. He hoped he was right and he didn't have any more surprises for his director—or for himself. He didn't think he'd fare well in another dust-up with Florence.

TEN

Back in his office, Chris dialled the number for Marvin's brother, but the call went unanswered. He was preparing to go to Alpha Unit when Gerald Reed appeared at his door. Chris had mentored his younger colleague when Gerald first joined the social work department, and Gerald in turn had supported Chris when he was recovering from his experience at Woodland Park. The two occasionally got together outside of work for hikes at Cypress Provincial Park or kayaking in North Vancouver's Deep Cove.

"I saw Threader the Shredder talking with you after the meeting. Everything okay with you?"

Chris rolled his eyes. "She said she tried getting you assigned to Marvin's case. Did you know that?"

"David mentioned it. He told her that you and

Marilyn work well as a team. He's getting pretty good at countering her moves. It's good to see. Speaking of which —" Gerald was smiling widely now "— how's it going with you and Stephanie?"

"We're good," Chris responded coyly.

"How good? Like 'friends with benefits' good or 'this is getting serious' good?"

"I'd say we're ..." Chris realized he hadn't talked openly about his feelings for Stephanie with anyone other than his counsellor. "Things are really good."

"I'll bet they are," Gerald laughed. "She's got this Jennifer Lawrence thing going on."

Chris shook his head. "She's got a Stephanie Rowe thing going."

"Wow. You really are smitten." Gerald picked up on his friend's awkwardness and laughed. "Don't mind me. I know how gutted you felt when your marriage ended. It's good to see you happy, that's all." His tone turned serious. "How're you feeling about the Owens interview? I know you didn't want your family connection to him out there for everyone to know."

Chris shrugged. "Not much I can do about it, is there?"

"He sure managed to get people riled up."

"Just what he wanted, an audience."

"I heard the lines lit up at the CBC, some taking Owens to task for his bullshit interview of manipulation, while others actually believe he's got a point and is a victim of 'the system,' if you can believe that. Even the Children's Ministry waded into the debate. Did you hear their statement?"

Chris shook his head. "What'd I miss?"

"They're in full damage control mode over what Owens said about the foster care program. They said they're proud of the program, and they threw out a bunch of numbers to back up their claims of the success they've had with kids in their care. Owens hit a nerve, even though he was talking out his ass."

Chris felt a headache coming on and tried to remember whether he had any ibuprofen left in his office.

"Oh, and that reporter, Chen, from the *Tribune?* She's been talking about her experience with Ray, about how she was 'creeped out' by her interview with him. She's tweeted so much about it, she's actually trending right now. It's a freaking gong show."

"Bloody hell! That's exactly the kind of reaction he was going for. He knew he'd ruffle feathers. Now he's sitting back laughing at the shitstorm he's created."

"Do you think there's any truth to what he said?"

"That's the thing about Ray. He's not stupid. He zeroes in on a vulnerable situation so he can capitalize on it. I'm sure he saw the news coverage on the child welfare system, the complaints about underfunding and understaffing. He took advantage, and you can bet it wasn't because he wanted to improve the situation. He grabbed an opportunity to stir the pot and see what would happen. Damn it!"

Chris' head was throbbing now and he badly wanted a drink. His alcohol consumption had increased substantially since his attack by Ray in Woodland Park. He was well aware, however, that when he drank anything stronger than beer, he could never stop at one.

"Hey, I'm sorry. I didn't mean to make things worse."

"It's not your fault, Gerald. That's what he does. I'd better get used to it because he sure as hell isn't going to stop anytime soon."

"How are *you* doing?"

Chris shrugged. "Days like this make it hard to forget about him. It's damn near impossible to do it!"

"Is it true you're seeing a counsellor?"

The question caught Chris by surprise, and he could feel his cheeks beginning to flush. He wasn't over-the-moon excited about having to see Nathaniel in the first place. He was even less thrilled that others knew.

"Hey, I think it's good," Gerald backpedalled. "You can always talk to me, too, if you want."

Chris nodded. "I know, and I appreciate it." He looked at his watch. "I guess I should be going."

Chris approached Alex at the Alpha Unit nursing station to get an update on Marvin.

"There's not much to tell you. He keeps to himself and doesn't say a word to anyone."

Chris told him about the call he had received from Marvin's brother. "Has anyone called the unit about him?"

"Not that I'm aware of, but we did get a fax from a doctor's office."

"Anything interesting?"

"There're a few reports. One said he was identified as having language problems as an infant and was referred to a child psychologist. That's all I've read so far. It's filed in his chart."

"Thanks. I'll take a look."

Chris flipped through Marvin's chart until he found a report with *Dr. William Bond, Family Physician* on the letterhead. Chris skimmed the contents. It was a consultation letter from April 2003 in which Bond requested a psychological assessment on Marvin. It stated that Marvin had been noted as a toddler to be developmentally delayed, with difficulty speaking and interacting with others, challenges that were formally identified in his kindergarten year. The report stressed the need for a speech/language therapist. Another report, this one from 2005, highlighted Marvin's functional deficits and his designation as a child with special needs. It, too, included a request for specialized educational services, such as one-to-one special assistants and a modified school program.

Chris looked for information about Marvin's family. He was rewarded for his efforts with a letter from 2012 from Dr. Bond to the Ministry of Child and Family Development in which Bond highlighted the need for specialized support for Marvin at home. The letter referred to Marvin's diagnoses of mental retardation and autism, and emphasized the fact that Marvin's mother, Eleanor Goodwin, was the primary caregiver and experiencing caregiver burnout. "Ms. Goodwin's efforts in providing care for her son have been nothing less than heroic, choosing to care for her son in her family home rather than placing Marvin in a group home. But in light of her own recent medical difficulties, a bulk of this responsibility has fallen to Marvin's brother who appears ill-equipped to meet this challenge. I implore you to consider providing respite support for the Goodwin family as well as a life-skills worker to assist Marvin with his Activities of Daily Living." According to the fax cover letter, this was the last known record for Marvin at Dr. Bond's office.

Chris was left with more questions. What had happened to Marvin between 2012 and now? Had he had any support or had he fallen through the cracks? What were his mother's medical problems? Was she still alive? And where was his father through all of this? Chris made a mental note to contact Dr. Bond's office with the hope of finding some answers. But for now, he'd try his luck with Marvin.

"Okay if I see Marvin in the interview room?" he asked Alex, handing back the chart.

"The room's free. Do you need anyone to join you?"

"No, I should be fine."

Chris walked to the interview room. Alex showed up a few minutes later with Marvin, who looked groggy.

"Did I wake you?" Marvin gave no response apart from rubbing his eyes.

"Do you remember me? I'm your social worker, Chris."

"Social worker, Chris."

"Yes. I just wanted to let you know your brother called me. Michael says hi." Marvin made brief eye contact.

Chris decided to return to the tactic that had worked before. "Can you write down your address?" he asked, handing Marvin a piece of paper and a pen.

Marvin scribbled something on the paper and passed it back to Chris. "Home," he said.

Chris read what looked to be a house number and street address. "Is this your home?"

"Home," Marvin repeated.

"That's good, Marvin. Does Michael live there with you?" No response. "How about anyone else?" Still nothing. "Is there anything else you want to write down for me?"

The young man pulled the paper to him and wrote some more before handing it back to Chris. It was another address. "Is this where your brother lives?"

"No! Home!" Marvin shouted. Chris couldn't tell if he was agitated or frightened. Either way, it was clear that he was done with questions. He looked away from Chris toward the door.

"Okay, I'll come back tomorrow. I'll walk you back to your room."

"Room." Marvin made brief eye contact with Chris before walking with him back to the nursing station to be escorted to his room.

Chris wasn't sure what had set Marvin off, but it seemed to have something to do with the second address. Why? Nonetheless, he took it as an encouraging sign that Marvin had shared more information with him. He was curious to find out what that information meant.

He had some time before the afternoon shift change for nurses and healthcare workers. He headed to Beta Unit to follow up on a call he'd received earlier from staff about another patient, Paul Butler. Paul had been admitted to IFP from Courtenay four months earlier. Back then he heard voices in his head and was convinced his computer was sending him disturbing messages. His mother couldn't get him admitted to her local hospital because he wasn't considered a risk to himself or others—that is, until he threw his computer out the window and threatened his mother. That was when Paul was admitted to IFP for a court-ordered assessment.

Dr. Stevenson had completed the assessment, with Chris helping by collecting information from Paul's mother. Courtenay Provincial Court found Paul not criminally responsible on account of a mental disorder, and he was now actively involved with treatment for his schizophrenia. Paul's treatment included taking daily medication, which helped take away the voices he'd been hearing as well as his bizarre thoughts about his computer. He also participated in psychosocial programs to learn more about his illness and steps toward maintaining wellness. In addition, Paul was attending vocational programs.

Chris entered the unit and said hi to one of his patients sitting in the dining room playing cards with his primary nurse. He saw Paul talking on the patients' phone. When Paul saw Chris, he looked excited and finished his call. "I was talking to my mother," he said as he approached Chris. Paul was dressed neatly in blue jeans and a black Nirvana T-shirt.

"How is your mother doing?" Chris asked.

"Good. She's planning to visit me later this week. We're wondering if I'll be able to go out with her for a few hours when she's here. She's going to call you."

"I'm really sorry, Paul. The hospital has just put a hold on passes in the community."

Paul's face fell. "Why?"

"Unfortunately, there was a situation where a patient was late returning to the hospital. An unauthorized absence was issued and —"

"Yeah, I knew about that. But how long before *I* can go?"

"I don't know, to be honest. There's going to be

a review. Hopefully, it won't take long. Whether it'll done before your mother visits, though, is doubtful. I can talk with your mother and explain the situation. All your outings with staff have gone well, so going out with your mother should be fine once day-leave privileges are reinstated. Do you want me to call her?"

"Yeah, I guess." Paul smiled feebly.

Chris felt immense guilt when it came to Paul. The young man had been seriously assaulted in the hospital three months earlier. It was widely suspected but never proven that Ray had executed the attack, and Chris was convinced Ray had targeted Paul simply because Paul was Chris' patient. Chris felt personally responsible for the attack.

He noticed that Paul looked pensive. "Is there something on your mind?"

Paul paused for a moment. "Can I ask you a question about uh ... Ray Owens?"

"What about him?"

"I read that interview he did with the paper. Thinking about him made me nervous so I did what I learned from my course and did some breathing exercises. But I get this feeling sometimes, like he's still going to come after me. I know it doesn't make sense, but that's how I feel."

Chris felt his own anxiety rising. "I know what you're saying. The important thing to remember is that he's no longer here. He's in custody and can't do anything to you now."

"What about you? Do you think he'll come after you again?"

It was an innocent question, Chris knew, but it still caught him completely by surprise. "I ... I don't think so." Even to himself he sounded unconvincing.

"Is it true he's your brother?"

"Half-brother," Chris corrected. "It's true." He paused, searching for the right thing to say to reassure them both. "The thing is, we can't live our lives in fear of people like Ray. That's what he wants us to do. We have to do our best to forget about him and move on."

"I try, but it's hard. Does it get any easier?"

"It does." Chris mentally winced at his lie. "It takes time, and some days are better than others, but it'll get better."

He told himself he had to believe this.

"Yeah, I guess so." Paul's face brightened. "Did you hear about the job I've got at the clubhouse?"

"I heard you were offered a few jobs. Tell me about it." Chris had received positive reports about Paul's involvement at the mental health clubhouse in New Westminster. Here participants were known as members as opposed to patients or clients, and activities focussed on strengths and abilities rather than illness. Paul had been going to the clubhouse with IFP staff for the past two months as part of a vocational services community outreach program.

"Well, I started in the maintenance unit, cleaning the floors, but then I tried the cooking unit, where I helped with lunches for the group, like in a restaurant. And now I'm in the communications unit, answering the phones."

"That's great. Which one do you like the most?"

"Well, I kinda like the communications unit because I've been getting some training on computers. But I've heard members have gone on to some pretty cool jobs at restaurants and hardware centres, so I'm thinking about that too."

"Sounds like you've got some options. That's really good to hear."

"Yeah, I like it there. I'm going later this morning. They haven't cancelled those outings, have they?" he asked in a panicked voice.

"No, that'll be fine because you're with staff," Chris assured Paul. "Well, I'll let you get on with your day. Talk soon."

Chris left the unit.

ELEVEN

On his drive home from work that afternoon, something about his earlier meeting with Marvin kept
gnawing at Chris. Why had Marvin reacted the way
he had to questions about the second address?

He reached into his pocket and retrieved the paper
with the addresses Marvin had written. Both were in
Vancouver. Maybe one or both would lead him to
Marvin's brother or other family members.

He was aware that going to either of the addresses
would be considered highly inappropriate. Standard
practice for conducting home visits involved communicating first with colleagues and the IFP security
department as a safety precaution, not to mention giving advance notice to the people he intended to visit.
He thought of Florence's earlier warning and figured

she'd tear a strip off him if she knew what he was planning. He didn't need the hassle.

Then he thought of Marvin, charged with murder, looking lost and scared in a place that was foreign to him. They had very little information about him, and Marvin didn't appear able to communicate his thoughts and feelings about the incident and what was going on for him. Chris wanted to help Marvin.

He decided to go for it.

On his smartphone, he Googled directions to the first address, the one Marvin had called his home. Twenty-five minutes later, he pulled up in front of the house on Vancouver's east side. His knocks on the front door went unanswered, and he didn't detect any movement inside the residence. A collection of newspaper flyers and mail reinforced his suspicion that the house was unoccupied. For how long, he didn't know, but from the paint peeling from the siding and the tattered bed sheet pulled over the living room window, it was clear the house had seen better days.

Marvin had called this place home, which left Chris wondering who was living there now. Was Marvin's mother still alive? Where was his brother? Using his phone, he searched Canada 411 and used the Reverse Address Lookup feature hoping to score a name associated with the home. No such luck. He strolled over to the house next door, figuring he could ask these questions of the neighbour, but no one answered that door either. He was considering going to another house—someone on the street had to be home—but then reminded himself that Marvin's incident was garnering a lot of media attention. Maybe people were just reluctant to get involved, particularly when a stranger without a uniform was knocking at the door. He took one last look up and down the street before deciding to leave.

Striking out at the first house strengthened his resolve to check the second one. He Googled the address and reached it minutes later. He stepped out of his Ranger and rang the doorbell. No response. He rang again. He looked up and down this street, too, for signs of activity, but as with the first address, he found none. Chris' Reverse Address Lookup revealed the house was registered to a Calvin Johnson. He Googled the name, but his search yielded no helpful results.

Perhaps people in this area were simply choosing to mind their own business. The thought nagged at him that this was advice he himself should probably consider following. He began to realize he'd embarked on a foolhardy venture without a plan, something he wouldn't normally do. If something were to happen to him, no one would know where he was or what he was doing, not to mention the fact that he'd broken the hospital's policy on conducting home visits. What did he expect to find anyway? He retreated to his truck and drove away.

He failed to notice the small surveillance camera mounted at the top right corner of the house under the eavestrough that had captured his every move from the moment he'd pulled up in front of the building.

After leaving the homes in Vancouver, Chris reached Deanna's house in New Westminster a few minutes past six.

Ann Marie excitedly opened the front door for him. "Can I have popcorn tonight?" She gave him a serious look, as though eternal happiness depended on her popcorn consumption.

"I don't know, Sweetie. Did you eat your supper?"

"She did," Deanna said, joining them.

"Well, if Mommy says it's okay with her, it's okay with me."

Ann Marie turned to her mother with a look of desperation on her face, forcing Deanna and Chris to laugh. "Okay." Deanna grinned.

"And pop, too?"

"Oh my gosh! What are we going to do with that sweet tooth of yours?"

"Just a little? Please, Daddy!"

"Fine. Just a little, though."

"She certainly has got you wrapped around her little finger." Deanna smiled.

Chris smiled in return. "What time should we be back?"

Ann Marie had already raced ahead to Chris'

truck, holding a Princess Ariana DVD in one hand and a Princess Ariana doll in the other.

"Eight thirty would be good." Deanna paused for a minute before adding, "You know, the next time, you could stay here to watch it."

"I just may take you up on that. See you in a while."

On the drive to Chris' apartment, Ann Marie talked happily to her father about her favourite scenes in the movie they were about to watch. When they arrived, she wasted no time in asking her father to prepare the microwave popcorn and pour the root beer while she organized their special seating arrangements. They cuddled up against each other.

Chris had shared Ann Marie's enthusiasm for the Princess Ariana movie the first three times he'd watched it with her. By now, he could recite key scenes almost as well as his daughter. His mind drifted off as he wondered what he would do if something happened to her. Not something. Someone. Ray Owens. He immediately tensed up and felt his grip on Ann Marie tighten.

"Are you okay, Daddy?"

"What? Oh, yes, Sweetie," he said, jolted back to reality. He exhaled deeply. "I love you so much, Ann. You know that, right?"

"I do. And I love you, too." She turned her attention back to her movie, joyfully oblivious to what her father had just gone through.

The evening came to an end too soon for Chris' liking, and judging from the frown on Ann Marie's face, she felt the same way. But he lifted her spirits, as well as his own, with talk about their weekend visit to the aquarium.

Ann Marie was sleeping by the time Chris pulled up in front of her home. He gently lifted her out of her seat and carried her toward the house. Deanna, wearing a burgundy silk dressing gown, met him at the front door. Together, they tucked Ann Marie into her bed and talked casually for a few minutes before Chris prepared to leave. To his mild surprise, Deanna hugged him, and he hugged her in return. It was a simple gesture, nothing more than a quick embrace. Still, since their separation, Deanna had limited her physical contact with Chris, so tonight's affection didn't go unnoticed.

As he drove to his empty apartment, he found himself thinking back on his marriage and his time in their once-happy home. He couldn't resist the what-if question that followed. What if he'd done a better job of listening to Deanna when she'd raised concerns about the impact of his work on their marriage? Staying late at work had become a habit for Chris, and when he'd finally get home, he'd be too physically and mentally exhausted to spend quality time with Deanna and Ann Marie.

He didn't want to repeat the mistake with Stephanie. Upon arriving home, he called her to say good night and to tell her he loved her.

Calvin Johnson punched in the number on his cell-phone. He lit a cigarette while waiting for a reply. "Some asshole's been snooping around my place." He took a long drag from his cigarette and slowly exhaled.

"Who is he?"

"Don't know, but I'm sure as hell gonna find out."

"What do you think he was doing there?"

"No clue. But if it's related to that Marvin kid, it's trouble."

"What if it is?"

"Then I'll take care of it."

TWELVE

The next day, Chris was no further ahead in solving the mystery surrounding Marvin. Who was he and how did he end up at a murder scene? Surfing the *Tribune*'s website from his office, Chris quickly realized he wasn't the only one searching for answers about Marvin.

He read the piece Lucy Chen had written that morning.

> The case, which has been dubbed "the Ice Cream Killer," has gripped the Lower Mainland, as the story of Alberto Bianchi's death appears to resonate with people for different reasons. Many have railed against what they see as another example of the city losing its war against rampant crime. The Letters to the Editor page of

this newspaper has been flooded by comments that boil down to one thing: what are people like Marvin Goodwin doing out on the street?

Opinions appear to be split as to whether Goodwin is a violent offender who deserves a stiff jail sentence or a vulnerable adult who requires specialized rehabilitation in a care facility.

There has also been no shortage of assigned blame, ranging from personal attacks against the Goodwin family for failing to provide Marvin with a proper upbringing, to criticism of the provincial government's controversial decision to close a tertiary psychiatric hospital without providing adequate community-support services for the mentally ill.

Chris had read enough; he closed the site. He needed to speak with Brandon about the case. He valued Brandon's opinion, not just as a police officer but as a trusted friend.

When he reached the sergeant, he outlined his concern. "Marvin's so anxious and timid, I can hardly get him to look at me. I'm finding it hard to see how he could kill someone. It just doesn't make any sense."

"Do you know how many times I've heard that over the years, Chris? The cold hard truth is all kinds of people do all kinds of crazy things for all kinds of reasons. And their reasons don't have to make sense. You of all people should know that, considering where you work. I don't think this one's too hard to understand. The guy has obvious mental problems, right? Something snapped and we all know the result."

"You're right, I've seen people do horrible things when they were influenced by voices in their head, acting in impulsive and irrational ways. But I don't see that with Marvin. He's done nothing to suggest that he acts impulsively. He's cognitively slow, sure, but he hasn't shown any evidence of responding to voices or acting on delusions. And he hasn't been violent while he's been with us. Besides, how the hell did he get himself out in the middle of nowhere in the first place? That road in Hope is a hundred and fifty kilometres away from his house in Vancouver."

"All right, Chris, I can see where you're going with this. If it'll make you feel any better, I'll ask around to see what's happening with the case. But I think you're going to be disappointed with what we find."

"Why do you say that?"

"Because I think you're a bit too close to this one. I know how hard you work with your patients and I understand why you want this kid to come out innocent, but from where I stand, the facts don't support it."

"Well, thanks for looking into it. I appreciate it, Brandon." He paused for a moment. "I also wanted to let you know Stephanie and I are going to Elizabeth's ceremony."

"That's great. I'll see you there."

After he hung up, Chris' thoughts remained on Marvin. *Was Brandon right? Was he too close to the case?*

Chris couldn't dwell on Marvin's case. He had other things to worry about, including making awkward phone calls to patients' families, explaining why patients' day leaves were on hold.

Chris wasn't looking forward to the call to Paul Butler's mother in particular. Susan Butler had put a lot of effort into planning her visit to IFP from her home in Courtenay, on the east coast of Vancouver Island. She'd made a reservation with BC Ferries to take her from Nanaimo to West Vancouver and then found a hotel for her nights in the Lower Mainland, and now Chris had to explain that the outing wasn't going to happen after all.

As he'd expected, she was disheartened. "Did Paul do something wrong?" she worried.

"No. He didn't do anything at all." Chris paused. What he wanted to say was that Paul was paying the price for a hypersensitive hospital administration concerned about public perception. "The hospital is undergoing a review to ensure sufficient safeguards are in place to maximize the success of all patient access to the community."

Chris made no attempt to hide the fact that he was reading, word for word, a scripted message from the IFP communications department. The fact that skilled mental health professionals were issued specific guidelines on communicating the cancellation of day leaves further added to his frustration of having to deliver this news.

Paul's mother took the news in stride and chose to continue with her planned visit, accepting that she would be limited to seeing her son in the hospital unit. Chris assured her that he'd seek permission for her to have flexible visiting times given that she was travelling from outside the Lower Mainland.

After making the arrangements with the unit for the visit, he glanced at his watch and realized that he would have to leave immediately if he intended to make it to Woodland Park in time.

As he drove to Woodland Park, Chris debated whether he was doing the right thing. The very idea of attending the park was triggering his PTSD symptoms. But he also appreciated the significance the park held for Elizabeth, so out of respect for her, he was forcing himself to attend the ceremony.

He was grateful that Stephanie was joining him for support. They met at the park entrance. As they started their hike into the interior of the park, painful memories flooded his mind: the gruesome sight of James Carrier's body, the torso blown apart; the jarring sensation of being shot in the shoulder; being forced by Ray to look down the barrel of his rifle, not knowing whether Ray was going to pull the trigger. Chris' heart started pounding so fast he thought he was going to pass out.

Recognizing that Chris was in the middle of a

panic attack, Stephanie held his hand and gently sat him down on the ground. "You're going to be okay, Chris. Just close your eyes, take a deep breath, and count to ten."

He followed her instructions.

"Now take another deep breath and slowly breathe out. This time, focus on what you hear around you." She stopped for a moment before continuing. "What do you hear?"

"A bird ... chirping in a tree."

"Where?"

"I don't know, close to us."

"Do you hear anything else?"

He listened more closely and was surprised as the trail seemed to come alive with birds singing all around him. Taking another deep breath, he opened his eyes and stood. Stephanie's grounding exercise had worked. His anxiety was slowly subsiding.

He soon felt strong enough to continue moving. "Thanks. Let's get this over with." They walked hand in hand into the park.

When he'd last been in the park, the ground had been covered with snow. Today the ground was bare, and the sunlight streaming through the trees reminded him of how much he had loved running on these trails. The smell of fresh leaves and the sound of singing birds gave evidence of the abundance of life in the park, partly countering the images of death and destruction ingrained in his memory.

After trekking for several minutes along the wooded trail, they were rewarded by reaching the entrance to a beautiful lake. They remained silent, taking in the tranquil sight of two ducks gliding across the still water, leaving a V-shaped pattern in their wake. At the far end of the lake, Chris saw a group of people gathered near a utility wagon holding a wooden park bench. Chris' moment of introspection was shattered by the solemn reality of why they were here.

Brandon was the first to greet them. "Glad you could make it." The sergeant hugged Stephanie before shaking Chris' hand.

"You been here long?" Chris asked.

"Twenty minutes or so." He leaned in and spoke to Chris quietly. "You okay?" When Chris nodded, he continued. "Elizabeth looks good, doesn't she?" He pointed out the two people standing next to her. "Her boyfriend, Robert, and Victoria, her mother."

Elizabeth did appear remarkably healthy and happy. Chris fought to shake away the image of the last time he'd seen her as a traumatized young woman with bloodshot eyes.

Elizabeth caught his gaze and smiled as she approached and gave him a warm embrace. After introductions all around, she said, "I'm so glad you could make it. This means so much to me and my mother."

"You look great," Chris said. "How are you feeling?"

"It's been hard at times, but my mom and I are seeing a therapist. And Robert's been great." She raised her left hand, calling his attention to a shiny ring on her finger. "I'm engaged!"

"Congratulations!" Chris hugged her again.

"I have you two to thank." Elizabeth looked at Chris and Brandon, tears welling up in her eyes.

Chris could feel his own eyes starting to tear up. "I wish I could have done more for your father."

Elizabeth led Chris away from the group. "Actually, there's something I've been wanting to ask you about my father," she said tentatively. "Do you mind?"

"Go on," Chris said with trepidation.

"You said you'd seen him walking in here before. Can you tell me about that?"

It took a moment for Chris to respond. "Well, at first, we'd pass without saying anything to each other. It was like we were both in our own little worlds. But one day, we were walking around this lake when there was a loud splashing sound. Right over there, in fact." Chris pointed to where he'd heard the noise. "It was a black bear thrashing around in the water. We watched it go ashore on the other side of the lake. It shook itself off and then disappeared into the bushes."

Chris stopped and looked at Elizabeth. Tears were streaming down her face, but she was smiling. "Your father and I laughed because we knew we'd shared a special moment. And from that day on, we updated each other on whether one of us had seen any wildlife on our walk." He stopped and briefly looked away from Elizabeth. "When I saw ... his body, I didn't want to believe it was him."

Elizabeth sniffled. "I know this is going to sound weird, but in a way, I'm glad it was you who found him, and not a total stranger."

"I can't tell you how many times I've wondered what would have happened if I'd been there earlier. Would it have made a difference?"

"My therapist calls those 'what if' questions, but there's nothing you could have done." She looked back at the little group. Her mother and fiancé were talking with Stephanie, but Brandon was making his way toward them. "I wanted to do something positive to remember my father, and that's how we came up with the idea of a bench to dedicate in his memory."

"Your mother is wondering if you wanted to start the ceremony now," Brandon joined in the conversation.

"Thank you," she said, and they walked back to rejoin the rest of the group. Elizabeth glanced around the lake. "Well, this looks like as good a place as any for the bench."

After they had arranged the bench where they wanted it, Elizabeth began to speak. "My father shared so much of his life with my mother and me, but ... well ... he was also a very private person." She wiped her eyes. "He kept his walks in this park for himself. He brought me here with him once, but my mother and I knew he loved to come here on his own. This park was special to him, which is why we chose it for a memorial."

Victoria Carrier then said a few words. The group mingled for a few minutes before Elizabeth, her mother, and Robert headed off, leaving Chris, Brandon, and Stephanie in the park.

"You want to cash in that beer I owe you?" Chris asked Brandon. "I know a decent pub around here. We can grab a bite to eat."

"Yeah, a beer would go down nice about now."

Conversation was light and pleasant as they enjoyed their time together. When Brandon left, Stephanie and Chris stayed behind to finish their discussion. Chris had already briefed Stephanie on his day at work and now asked about hers.

"I had a good one. I'm really excited about the group I'm running." She proceeded to tell Chris about her group at the West Coast Correctional Centre, which focussed on inmates accepting personal responsibility for the actions that led to their incarceration. "The great majority of these guys have experienced adverse childhood events ranging from physical and sexual abuse to suffering other forms of trauma at a young age, such as the death of a family member. This isn't an excuse for their actions; it's actually the opposite. It's about helping them understand their abuse so they can learn skills to stop their cycle from repeating." Stephanie's passion about her work was one of the many things Chris loved about her. As he listened intently, he also became aware of a bubbling anxiety.

"Are you okay, Chris?"

"I'm sorry, Stephanie. I couldn't help but think about Ray's threats against you. I know you're safe there, but it doesn't stop me from worrying about you."

"I know. But like I've said, he's on a locked unit, in a completely different building from mine. I never enter his building and there's no way he'd enter mine. He'd never be a candidate for my group, either, because he never accepts personal responsibility for his actions, just blames everyone else. Like that interview he did, blaming the Children's Ministry, or blaming a mental illness we both know he doesn't have. You have to trust me, Chris. I'm safe, and I know what I'm doing."

Chris exhaled slowly. "I do, Stephanie. I trust you completely. It's my issue, I know. I'm really glad you like your work. I can see how good you are at it."

"Now you're sucking up," she said playfully. "Enough talk about work. Let's meet back at my place and do something fun."

THIRTEEN

Ray shuffled into the large guard-supervised visiting room at the West Coast Correctional Centre. Located in Abbotsford, the facility housed male inmates still before the court and awaiting trial as well as sentenced inmates. Ray was mildly curious to know who'd come to see him because he didn't get many visitors. He didn't recognize the portly balding man, but the perfectly tailored suit and crocodile-skin Oxfords told Ray the guy hadn't stumbled here on a whim.

The man stood up from his seat and extended his hand. "Good afternoon, Mr. Owens."

Ray didn't bother shaking his hand, choosing instead to grunt a greeting in response. They both sat.

"Mr. Owens, I read the piece you did with the *Tribune*. I must say, my friend, it was entertaining. I—"

"Quit the bullshit. You ain't my friend. Who are you?" Ray growled impatiently.

"Well, that depends on you. I could be your lawyer." The man looked across the table at Ray, waiting for a response. He didn't get one, so he continued. "Two counts of murder, one count of attempted murder." He raised an eyebrow. "That could set you back quite a while. You'd come out with less hair than I have."

"I don't need no stupid lawyer. I'm representing myself."

"And how's that working out for you?" The man looked pointedly at the high-security room they were sitting in.

"How would you do any better?" Ray shot back.

"Oh, I hear there are certain creature comforts a man comes to appreciate in settings like this. And you've got a court date coming up. From what I understand, the Crown is keen to get your case to trial as soon as possible. I don't mind telling you I know my way around the court, and I've learned a few tricks along the way."

He leaned forward and spoke in a quiet voice to avoid being overheard by the guard. "I could delay your trial for months. Would that interest you?" He looked Ray squarely in the eye. "Or would you prefer to take your chances on finding your own way out of this mess you've gotten yourself into?"

"It's Ryder's fault I'm in this shithole!" Ray

exploded in a rage. He collected himself before the guard intervened. "But don't worry about me. I'll get by fine without your help."

The man continued to speak softly, unmoved by Ray's tirade. "What if I told you the client I represent shares a common interest when it comes to Mr. Ryder?"

Ray sat up ramrod straight. "Who're you talking about?"

"That's a detail we don't need to go into right now. All you need to know is that this client would be prepared to retain my services to represent you. All I need to know is whether you're interested."

"I'll tell you what I need: a psych assessment to say that I'm criminally nuts. Can you manage that?"

"Well, Mr. Owens, I can certainly look into it."

Ray sat back in his chair and stroked the grey stubble on his chin. "Those mindfuckers at IFP called me opportunistic, like it was a bad thing. I call it survival. If your client is willing to pay my legal fees while I get to make Ryder's life a living hell, who am I to say no?"

"I'll take that as a yes, then. Good, we have the makings of a deal." The man stood up, reached into his pocket and pulled out a business card with the name *Phillip Bernum* printed in bold. "We'll talk soon." The lawyer motioned to the guard to escort him from the room.

FOURTEEN

Sitting alone in his worn-out chair in his worn-down house, Maurice Ryder stared listlessly at the television. He wasn't concentrating on the show; he never did. It simply served to pass the time. He gulped back one mouthful of rum, then another.

A solitary tear trickled down his cheek. *What the heck?* He patted at the wetness on his face, then looked at his wet finger with surprise. It had been years since the one time he'd allowed himself to cry: the day his wife had died, to be precise. The day he lost Fiona was the day he exiled himself to his own hell, cutting out everything and everyone that had once mattered to him, including his son. But recent developments had made him realize his opportunities to see Chris again were limited, and the realization affected him in a way that surprised him now.

A lucid thought entered his alcohol-soaked brain, and he considered the implications of actually talking with his son and telling him the truth about his mother. *I owe Chris that much.*

FIFTEEN

Chris drove to work the next morning with pleasant thoughts on his mind from his previous evening with Stephanie. His workday started with a team meeting on Alpha at nine a.m. These meetings were attended by psychiatrists, nurses, healthcare workers, a family practitioner, and a pharmacist as well as social workers. Today's meeting included an in-service from Dr. Becky Thomson, a family practitioner, on how to administer Naloxone, a medication used to block the effects of opioids, especially in cases of overdose such as fentanyl. A plan was developed to identify patients at risk on Alpha so that they too could be given the education as well as a Naloxone kit prior to their discharge.

The remainder of Chris' day was fairly routine: team meetings with his patients and follow-up telephone calls with patients' families, particularly those impacted by the moratorium on day leaves. He talked diplomatically about the merits of the review, but as the day wore on, he found himself becoming increasingly preoccupied with thoughts about his evening session with his counsellor. Before leaving the hospital, he texted Stephanie. "Seeing Nathaniel. Love you."

Chris initially thought today's session would focus on his recent return to Woodland Park for Elizabeth's ceremony. He'd already briefed Nathaniel when he'd called to confirm their appointment.

But something happened on the way to the counsellor's office in downtown Vancouver that was an even bigger worry for him now, and he wasted no time in expressing his concern. "I think I was followed here."

"Followed? What makes you think that?"

"I saw a black Expedition behind me at a stop-light on Burrard Street. It stood out because it had tinted windows, the ones that prevent you from seeing inside. I saw it again about five minutes later on Granville Street. It looked like it was keeping a distance but not losing me, almost like he wanted me to know he was following me."

"You think the driver *wanted* you to know he was following you?"

"I'm not sure." Chris gave the counsellor a surprised look. "You think I'm making a big deal over this, don't you? You think I'm paranoid?"

"I don't know if I'd go so far as to say paranoid. But I think it might be good to keep an open mind to other alternatives. For example, is it possible the vehicle was simply heading in a similar direction and had nothing at all to do with you?"

Chris nodded somewhat grudgingly.

"But," Nathaniel continued, "the bigger question is why you think someone would be following you."

Chris reflected for a moment. "I guess I've been questioning people and things going on around me lately."

"Can you elaborate?"

Chris sighed but otherwise remained silent.

"Chris, it's common, when people experience trauma, to feel less secure than they normally would, as they adjust to their new normal."

"Maybe. But I don't feel like I'm in control these days." He looked away from Nathaniel.

"When you say 'control,' what exactly are you referring to?"

"Control of my emotions, for starters. My sleep is also shot to hell. And ever since Ray, I've been worried about the people around me, especially Ann Marie, Deanna, and Stephanie."

"But Ray's in jail, and you've had no contact with him for over three months. Correct?"

"I know, but I can't shake the feeling that we're not done, that *he's* not done. And if anything ever happened to my family, it'd be my fault."

Nathaniel looked confused. "How would it be your fault?"

Chris paused, unsure if he wanted to be dragged any further into this conversation because of where it might lead him. But he also believed this question was at the root of his present problems. "Because I didn't kill Ray when I had the chance." He exhaled deeply. "Wow, I can't believe I said that."

"I'm not sure I understand."

"You have no idea how much time I spend reliving those moments in Woodland Park: Ray with the rifle on me, me with the rifle on him. It goes on and on like a continuous loop in my head. But I could have ended it all when I held the rifle on him. A simple pull of the trigger and, boom, it's all over. No more Ray, no more problems."

"You wanted to shoot Ray?"

"I did. And it would have been justifiable self-defence. He shot me." Chris pointed to his right shoulder and winced at the remembered pain. "And I know he was going to kill me as soon as I led him to his cellphone." His mind drifted back to the memory of Ray's contorted face, and he winced again.

"But you didn't shoot him." Nathaniel brought Chris back into the moment.

"No. And it's my biggest regret, my biggest mistake."

"I don't see it as a mistake, Chris. I see it as confirmation of all your good qualities as a compassionate human being. That even after you were injured and had the chance to do the same to the person who injured you, you chose not to."

"That all sounds well and good. But the reality is, he's not going to stop until he's broken me. Until he's killed everyone I love. He said it, and it's the one thing he's said that I believe."

"How often would you estimate you relive those moments in the park?"

"There's not a day goes by that I don't think about it at some point. And that's when I'm awake. It's even worse when I'm trying to sleep. It's like I can't turn my brain off. I wake up in the middle of the night from a nightmare." He suddenly remembered something he had wanted to tell Nathaniel. "I had one last night that was pretty messed up."

"I'm interested in hearing it." Nathaniel leaned forward.

Chris took a deep breath and exhaled slowly. "I'm standing on the ground, looking up at someone tethered to a hot air balloon. I don't see a face, but I can tell it's one of my patients and I'm holding the line as he goes farther up into the sky. The next thing I know, the line slips through my fingers and I've lost sight of him. I start panicking that he's gone forever and that it's my fault for letting go of the line. That's when I woke up with my sheets soaking wet." He laughed nervously. "Told you it was screwed up."

"What does it mean to you?"

"Well, obviously it's about work. The hospital's been in the news a lot recently. I'm working with the guy who's been charged with killing that ice cream vendor. You know the one?"

Nathaniel nodded. "I've read about it."

"Seems everyone has. Now, I totally sympathize about what happened to Mr. Bianchi. I really do. It was horrible, and I feel bad for his family. But the way Marvin's been portrayed has also been horrible. The attacks on him in the paper have been vicious. He'd be swinging from a tree right now if some people had their way. They're calling for him to be locked away for the rest of his life. There's this perception that he deliberately planned this killing in cold blood, when the reality is that he can't even plan his next meal, for God's sake."

"It sounds like this case has affected a lot of people on a deep, personal level, including you."

"Well, yeah. I guess what really bothers me is that it's not just Marvin who's affected. A case like his reinforces every prejudice out there toward people living with mental health challenges. If we were talking about some other kind of illness, there'd be understanding and support. But when someone in this situation comes into conflict with the law, there's this skepticism, this feeling that they're faking illness to avoid jail. I mean, there *are* people like that —" *like Ray*, he thought "—but they're few and far between."

"Sounds like you've been struggling with public perception that stigmatizes the mentally ill and it's finding its way into your dreams. Going back to your dream for a moment, what do you make of the image of the patient flying away from you?"

"I don't know. What do *you* think it means?"

"To me, this dream taps into your feelings of being responsible for your patients and their actions. The fact of the matter is, there's a limit to how responsible you can be for the actions of any other person." Nathaniel looked squarely at Chris before continuing. "Whether it's Ray or one of your patients, there's only so much you can do and only so much responsibility you should bear."

"I just hate looking over my shoulder all the time, worrying if they're safe when they're out of my sight."

"When who's out of your sight? Your patients or your family?"

"Both, actually. On the one hand, I feel deeply connected with Stephanie, but I also fear that I'm putting her safety in jeopardy by continuing with our relationship. The question is, how do I get past this … this fear?"

"You're taking a positive step right now by talking about it. Those feelings won't go away overnight, but you'll get there."

"I hope so."

"Let's go back to what you said about work. Have you had difficulty concentrating or keeping focussed on a given task?" Chris shook his head. "Have there been instances where you've acted in ways that are uncharacteristic?"

"No," Chris lied. He didn't feel like disclosing his recent trip to the addresses Marvin had provided out of fear his judgement would rightly be called into question. "I know where you're headed with this. You're checking for the severity of my PTSD symptoms."

"And?"

"And, well, yeah, there's what happened when I returned to Woodland Park."

"What about your alcohol intake?"

"I have it under control," he said, as if trying to convince himself. "The main thing is my sleep: getting to sleep, staying asleep, and not waking up from crappy nightmares all the time. It's at the point where I dread going to sleep."

"As we've talked about before, sleep problems are common with PTSD. It stands to reason that getting good-quality sleep is going to be critical in addressing your symptoms."

"I want—I *need*—to get some decent sleep." He hesitated before going on. "It's also becoming an issue with Stephanie and me."

"How so?"

"Because waking up in the middle of the night, soaking wet with sweat, wakes her up, too. She hasn't complained, but it's embarrassing, and it's getting to the point where I don't want to sleep in the same bed with her. It sucks." Chris shook his head in frustration.

"Would you be willing to keep a dream diary so we can discuss your dreams during our meetings?"

"A dream diary?"

"Are you familiar with Imagery Rehearsal Therapy?"

"No."

"Imagery Rehearsal involves writing down your dreams and nightmares, particularly your recurring ones. Over time, you'll write and rehearse new endings to those nightmares, but endings that are less traumatic for you. People using this strategy have reported a lower frequency of nightmares, so this may be helpful with yours, particularly the one involving Ray and his rifle. What do you think?"

"It's worth a try."

"That's good to hear." The counsellor paused, as if searching for the most tactful way to express himself. "Look, Chris, I wouldn't be doing my job if I didn't point out a few things you've said that concern me."

Chris shifted his weight in his chair, feeling uncomfortable. "What did I say?"

"For starters, you commented that you thought someone was following you, without any concrete evidence to back that up. I think you may be experiencing what is known as hyperarousal, a constant feeling of being in danger. Given your experience, this would be understandable."

Chris felt his ears getting hot. He swiped a finger across his forehead to remove a bead of sweat.

"And I asked you about your alcohol intake because you previously acknowledged that after you were attacked by Ray, your drinking patterns changed. You switched from having an occasional beer to regularly drinking rum to excess. Yet today you avoided answering my questions about your drinking altogether. I point this out because it's important to acknowledge your symptoms."

Chris reflected for a brief moment. "You're right. I'll try to be more open with you."

"That's a good note to end on."

As Chris walked out the building, he received a text from Stephanie. "How was it?"

"Good, but exhausting," he responded, adding a tired emoji.

On the drive home, Chris drummed his fingers on the steering wheel, feeling good about his session with Nathaniel. He noticed a black Expedition SUV a few cars behind him. It was far enough behind him that he couldn't make out the licence plate, but he was sure it was the same one he'd seen earlier and felt sick to his stomach at the prospect of being followed. He slowed down before turning right on Burrard Street, as a test, and the Expedition kept going straight.

That had him reflecting on his earlier conversation with Nathaniel. What objective evidence did he have for thinking he was being followed? He wasn't sure anymore.

SIXTEEN

Another restless night left Chris feeling ill-prepared to handle his next day's demands. He walked into his office and checked his voicemail. The number of messages waiting for him was generally an accurate indicator of how his day would turn out. Today's nine messages told him he was in for a rough morning. Setting his messenger bag down, he powered up his computer and started playing back the missed calls.

He soon knew why people were trying so insistently to reach him. Marvin had been involved in an altercation with staff the previous evening and was now in seclusion.

Seclusion rooms were used as a last resort when a patient was considered unsafe to remain on an open unit with his peers and less restrictive options had been exhausted. This was something that usually occurred when the patient was unable or unwilling to follow staff direction and was deemed a risk to himself and others.

He rushed to Alpha Unit. Spotting Alex, he asked what had led to Marvin's admission to seclusion.

"He had a meltdown," Alex said in exasperation. In response to Chris' confused look, he added, "A new patient saw the newspaper on the table, didn't know it was Marvin's, and took it. Marvin freaked out, started shouting 'Home' over and over and knocking over chairs."

"Anyone hurt?"

Alex shook his head. "We called Code White and stopped it before it got any further. But we couldn't reason with him at all. Dr. Stevenson's on her way here to see whether he's settled down enough to come out of seclusion."

Code White was an emergency staff response to aggression, be it patient against patient or patient against staff member. Staff responders were trained in violence de-escalation techniques as well as safe practices in containing a violent situation.

"All of this over a paper? What are the chances of the unit getting two papers, so we can guarantee Marvin gets his own?"

"You know how it goes, Chris. Filling out the paperwork, processing the request. It'll take a week before we see anything. Meanwhile ..."

"It's the *Tribune* he likes. What if I bring in my own for the next few days until the unit gets its second order? I'll bring it down first thing tomorrow, okay?"

He nodded to Dr. Stevenson, who'd entered the nursing station and picked up Marvin's chart to review the nursing notes.

"Worth a shot. But he's gonna have to do better than this. He can't be exploding on us."

"We'll tell him that now," Dr. Stevenson said as she closed the chart and joined the conversation.

Alex gestured patience. "We're gonna have to wait a few minutes. I don't have enough staff right now to see Marvin. We're busy with our new admission in another seclusion room." Alex explained that a patient named Tim Spirling, admitted the previous evening from Surrey Pre-trial Centre, had verbally attacked another patient without provocation during supper. When staff stepped in to intervene, Tim could not be de-escalated. He had shouted incoherently about the Illuminati and lunged at a nurse. Code White was activated, and nurses and healthcare workers from surrounding units attended Alpha to provide additional support to contain the situation.

"Last night Tim flooded the toilet, and this morning he stripped naked and defecated all over the floor. Dr. Stevenson ordered a shot of Acuphase, which we're giving now. Hopefully it'll calm him down." As Alex said this, Chris heard the seclusion room door close and a collection of staff entered the now-crowded nursing station. "How'd it go?" Alex asked.

A nurse named Danielle shook her head in disbelief. "My hands are still shaking. I could hardly hold the needle still. We're going to have to move Tim to another seclusion room to give house-keeping staff time to clean the room. There's crap everywhere."

Over his years at IFP Chris had seen his share of patients in the throes of an acute psychotic episode. It never ceased to amaze him to see that extreme compared to the same individual once his health had been restored through treatment and rehabilitation. He hoped this would soon be the case with Tim.

Alex looked toward Dr. Stevenson. "We can go see Marvin now."

They walked through the corridor toward Marvin's seclusion room. Chris had to hold his nose to block out the stench as they passed Tim's room. Alex knocked on Marvin's door. "Marvin, Dr. Stevenson's here to see you. Please stay on your mattress. Do you understand?"

Marvin didn't respond, but he remained seated on the bare mattress and made no attempt to get up as the door opened. Dr. Stevenson, Alex, another nurse named Will, and Chris walked into the stark room with bland eggshell-coloured cinder-block walls. Chris noticed the food on Marvin's breakfast tray hadn't been touched.

Chris always felt uneasy inside the seclusion rooms. He couldn't imagine being confined to one, left alone with nothing but a mattress, blanket, toilet, and sink. He reminded himself that for many patients in a highly agitated state, the lack of stimulation in a quiet room actually helped de-escalate the situation.

"Good morning, Marvin. I understand you had a hard time last night," Dr. Stevenson said. "How are you feeling now?"

Marvin slowly looked at each person in the room, although Chris had the impression that Marvin kept his gaze on him for a split second longer than anyone else. "Home."

"You want to go home," Dr. Stevenson acknowledged in a direct but soft voice. "We understand and we're working on that, but you're going to have to listen to staff. They're here to help, so if something is bothering you, you need to tell the nurses." She paused for a moment, considering Marvin's cognitive challenges and what she was asking of him. "Or write it down for staff."

"Write down," Marvin repeated.

"Yes, that's good. So, for example, if you can't find your paper, write that down for staff, and they will help you find it. Do you want to come out of this room?"

Marvin nodded. "Out."

"Okay, that's good. First, we'll give you some time to get a shower. Then we'll see how you do at snack time with the other patients. If you handle that without any problem, you can return to your room this afternoon. Is that clear?"

He nodded again. "Clear."

"Do you have any questions?"

Marvin slowly shook his head.

"Does anyone have any questions or anything to say to Marvin?"

No one had anything to add.

"Okay, then. Marvin, I'll come by to see you later this afternoon."

"Afternoon."

The group left the room and congregated in the nursing station to discuss Marvin's return to the unit.

"We're not doing him any favours here," Dr. Stevenson scowled. "He has a number of ritualistic behaviours, and as we've seen, he copes very poorly to changes to his routine and environment. He needs a place where an individualized care plan can be consistently carried out. Not a unit with twenty-one other guys and new people coming and going every day."

Chris knew Marilyn was referring to the Neuro-Psych program, which was designed to work with patients with challenges similar to Marvin's, but that unit wouldn't be an option for Marvin until his court matter was resolved. "I placed a call with Community Living Society," Chris responded. "They'll have to do a review to confirm that Marvin's needs fall under their mandate, and there's likely going to be a long waiting list, if he is approved. But I've asked them to start the intake process. I'll keep you updated."

"Good," Dr. Stevenson responded. "We need a behavioural consultant to help develop a care plan for Marvin while he's here. We need to identify his triggers as well as develop strategies to de-escalate Marvin when he's getting frustrated. Then we need to ensure all staff are familiar with the care plan and carry it out consistently. I'll have an order available for Ativan to help calm him when he's starting to get agitated. I'll also talk with Psychology to see if there's anything they can suggest. They're already due to see him for a neuro-psych assessment."

The rest of Chris' day was less dramatic: working on a social history for a patient who'd recently been found not criminally responsible on account of a mental disorder, in preparation for his upcoming Review Board hearing, and callbacks to a number of his patients' families, mostly dealing with the fallout from the hold on community passes. The day flew by.

Despite having reason to feel good about his productivity, Chris felt fatigue and a quiet despair as he drove home. He couldn't shake the image of Marvin losing control on the unit and he started to second-guess his assessment of his patient. If Marvin's impulse control was so poor over something as trivial as missing a newspaper, could he have been provoked into a murderous rage, as the criminal charge against him suggested? He wondered if Brandon was right about him being too close to the case.

SEVENTEEN

Chris was excited Saturday morning as he and Stephanie drove to Deanna's home to pick up his daughter for their outing. Halfway up the walkway to the house the front door swung open and a jubilant Ann Marie bounded down the walk, her silky brown hair bouncing as she ran, and jumped into his arms. "Where's Stephanie?"

"She's waiting in the truck, Sweetie."

"Can I go see her?"

"Sure. I just need a minute to talk to Mommy and we'll be on our way."

Deanna met him at the front entrance. "She's been looking out the window for you the last thirty minutes." She smiled. "What time do you think you'll be back?"

"Is six okay?"

Deanna nodded. "You can always call if you're running late. I'll be home anyway." She waved at her daughter, who was looking back at her parents with a wide grin. "Have a good time."

Chris saw the smile leave her face. "Is everything okay?"

"Yeah, just a little tired."

Her response didn't sound convincing to Chris and he wondered if it had to do with Stephanie's presence. "You have any plans with Walter?"

"No, not today."

Whatever the problem was, Deanna didn't want to talk about it. "Okay, well, we're off. See you later."

As they drove into Vancouver, Ann Marie listed all the things she wanted to see at the aquarium. She excitedly asked Chris three times whether she could order waffles at the restaurant, and he joked each time that he wasn't sure if they still served them. When they finally arrived, Ann Marie made a point of leading Stephanie inside. "This and Wilbur's are me and my daddy's favourite restaurants in the whole world!"

"Well, in that case, I feel very lucky to be here," Stephanie responded with enthusiasm. "What do you want to order?" she added, even though she knew by now what the answer would be.

"Waffles! They come with strawberries for dipping in chocolate and whipped cream. I like them best."

"Yum! I think I'll order the same."

Ann Marie giggled in delight. "Daddy always gets the sausage and eggs, but I think the waffles are better."

"Sounds like he doesn't know what he's missing."

Chris listened to their cheerful banter and grinned. He was nervous the first few times Stephanie joined them on their Saturday outings, wondering how his daughter would get along with her. Truth be told, Ann Marie had appeared quiet and reserved toward Stephanie during their early visits, but by now it was apparent they were beginning to forge a bond of their own. Stephanie was a natural around children.

When their meals arrived, Ann Marie showed Stephanie her special technique for dipping strawberries in chocolate sauce. She laughed at Stephanie's messy attempt to do the same. "You've got chocolate on your chin!"

"I guess I need more practice."

"I've had lots of practice."

"Practice makes perfect."

"That's what Daddy says!"

"I do." Chris looked at Ann Marie. "Maybe we'll have to bring Stephanie here more often so she gets better at dipping the strawberries. What do you say?"

"Yes!" Ann Marie shrieked.

"Uh-oh. Looks like the sugar's kicking in." Chris grinned. "So tell me, Sweetie, what are you looking forward to the most at the aquarium?"

"The sea otters, no, the sea lions!"

"I've never seen the sea lion show, so that's what I'm looking forward to," Stephanie said.

"I want to show you," Ann Marie declared. "But we can't get too close or we'll get wet," she cautioned.

Chris locked eyes with Stephanie and they both smiled.

They left the restaurant and drove to the aquarium in Vancouver's Stanley Park. True to her word, Ann Marie took Stephanie by the hand and they both walked eagerly to grab the best vantage point for the show. As it began, Chris couldn't tell who was more excited. They spent the next two hours after the show touring the facility and exploring the vast array of creatures native to the West Coast.

Chris was pleasantly exhausted as they exited the aquarium and their eyes adjusted to the bright sunny afternoon.

"Can we walk along the seawall, Daddy?"

"Where do you get the energy?" Chris laughed and looked at Stephanie, who nodded. "Let's do it."

Approaching the harbourfront area, they were met by hundreds of tourists looking happily lost after disembarking from a massive cruise ship. They stopped to take in the spectacle of seaplanes coming and going against the backdrop of the majestic North Shore Mountains while seagulls soared through the blue, cloudless sky.

After their walk, they decided to go for a drive to visit a few of Chris' old neighbourhoods in Vancouver.

The first was an apartment building not far from the Main Street SkyTrain station. Chris had lived there for a couple of years when he was in his mid-twenties, and Ann Marie pleaded with him to tell Stephanie the story about the mouse that had taken up residence with him during one wet winter. Ann Marie squealed in mock horror as her father recalled the noise it made running over his tile floor in the middle of the night.

Next he drove past the ritzy apartment building in Kitsilano where he'd moved as a response to his previous rodent-infested suite. He had fond memories of ordering pizza from the Flying Wedge on Cornwall Avenue and running the route from Kitsilano Beach to Jericho Beach. He recalled, too, the countless hours he'd spent at Kitsilano watching boats sailing in the sparkling waters of Burrard Inlet.

Sharing this moment with his daughter and Stephanie filled Chris with contentment. He thought back to the last time he'd been at Kitsilano Beach and his mood suddenly turned somber when he realized it had been after visiting his patient Paul Butler in the hospital after Paul had been brutally assaulted by Ray.

Even in my most joyful moments, Chris thought bitterly, *the mere thought of Ray shatters my serenity and crushes my sense of security.* It took a great deal of effort, using breathing exercises and replacing negative thoughts with positive ones, but eventually he managed to banish Ray from his mind for the moment and returned to pleasant thoughts of his loved ones.

By the time Chris returned to Deanna's house, Ann Marie had fallen asleep in the truck. He carried his daughter to her room and updated Deanna on their day. Now he was looking forward to spending his evening with Stephanie.

Chris lay beside Stephanie in her bed.

"I had a good time, Chris."

"Thank you, thank you very much," Chris said in a bad Elvis impersonation. "You weren't too bad yourself."

"Not that! I mean today, with Ann Marie." Stephanie playfully hit him on the arm.

"I know," he laughed. "You were great with her. She really likes you."

"I like her, too. She's a good kid." She suddenly became silent.

"What's wrong?"

"Nothing. I was just thinking about something, that's all."

"Come on, what is it?"

"I saw how great you were with Ann Marie. She adores you, Chris. You're a good father. And I really felt like we were a family today. It was nice."

"It was nice. You'd be a great mother."

She looked Chris in the eye. "That's been on my mind a lot lately, being a mother, having a family. I think we'd make good parents."

"You're thinking about a baby?"

"Well, yeah. Have *you* thought about it?"

"Not really."

"Why not?"

Chris thought she sounded slightly defensive. "I don't know. Maybe because I'm happy with the way things are right now."

"But how would you feel if we did have a baby? I don't mean right now, obviously there's too much going on right now, but some day. I'm not getting any younger."

Chris realized their discussion had quickly shifted from a light, hypothetical conversation to a serious one. "I hadn't really thought about being a new father again. Are you saying you want to get pregnant?"

Stephanie appeared flustered now. "The way you ask makes me feel like you think it's wrong."

"It's not *wrong*, of course not. I'm just, well, surprised, that's all."

"Why does it surprise you?"

"I guess I thought maybe we'd move in together first before we took things any farther than that. I mean, we haven't really talked about it."

"I drop hints all the time but you don't ... oh, just forget I mentioned it." Stephanie looked away.

Chris put his arms around her. "I love you, Stephanie. I just get, I don't know ... scared."

"Scared of what?"

"Of being responsible for someone so fragile,

making sure nothing bad ever happens. It scares me sometimes, thinking back to all that's happened. I wouldn't want to go through that again."

"Are you talking about Ray?"

Chris reluctantly nodded.

"But he's in jail." Stephanie gave him a bewildered look. "That part of your life is over, Chris. We have a whole new life ahead of us now. It's going to be fine. Okay?"

"Okay." He got out of bed and started getting dressed.

"You're not staying?" She frowned. "Did my talk about wanting a family frighten you?"

"No. Sorry. I want to stay—really, I do. I just don't think I'll be able to sleep and I don't want to keep you up, too. I'll call you when I get home." He kissed her on the forehead. "Love you."

Chris' gloomy feeling followed him home that night. He grabbed a Granville Island Pilsner from the fridge, shuffled his iPod, and crashed on his futon. Pike's "Convicts in the Sky" echoed through his apartment.

The ringing phone distracted him from his beer. He wanted to ignore it, but he thought it might be Stephanie. He was feeling guilty for bailing on their evening and knew he owed her an apology.

It wasn't Stephanie.

"Uh ... it's Maurice. Have you got a minute?"

Talking to his father wasn't something Chris felt prepared to do. The man's voice sounded tired. Chris figured he'd probably been drinking. "How'd you get my number?"

"Your Aunt Mary."

"Why are you calling?

"Uh ... well, I was hoping to see you. There's a few things I need to say."

Chris felt his cheeks burning. "You didn't seem interested in talking with me the last time I saw you." He took a gulp of his beer and put the bottle down, looking at it with disdain. Suddenly he wanted something much stronger to drink.

"I know we didn't get on very well last time. We both said some things ..." Maurice hesitated. "But I was hoping you'd give me another chance. There are a few things I need to square up with you."

Chris marched into the kitchen, still holding the phone, and snatched the bottle of Captain Morgan from the cupboard and a cola from the fridge. He spilled rum onto the counter and let the cola overflow the glass. Ignoring the mess, he took a large mouthful.

His father was still talking. "Chris, there's a reason I'm calling, if —"

"I really don't feel like talking right now. I'm sure you know the feeling. Maybe tomorrow." He hung up.

After Chris texted Stephanie to say good night, the rest of the night was a blur.

EIGHTEEN

Chris' head felt like it had spent the night in a vise grip. He was relieved to have a day to recover before returning to work.

But he was also mad at himself for the way he'd treated Maurice. Receiving a phone call from his father had caught him off guard, and he felt bad for shutting him down the way he had. In the sober light of day, he was curious why his father had wanted to talk. There had been a time in Chris' life when he would have given anything to receive a call from him, or any indication at all that he mattered to the man. So why was Maurice calling now?

He was unsure of his next move, feeling nervous about how Maurice would react if Chris called him so soon after last night's debacle. He decided to wait a few days to let things cool down. Then he'd call his Aunt Mary to see if she knew anything about why Maurice wanted to speak with him in the first place.

In the meantime, he had other pressing concerns. His phone rang, and the chiming noise intensified the aching in his head.

It was Stephanie. "You sound awful."

"I feel awful." He told her about his call from Maurice and reluctantly filled her in on his drinking binge.

Stephanie was silent for a moment. "Did he say why he was calling?"

"I didn't give him much of a chance." Now it was his turn to pause. "I feel pretty crappy about it now, but last night, I was just too mad to talk." He told her about his plan to contact Maurice in a few days.

"How much did you drink?"

"Too much." He promised himself that he'd throw out the rest of his hard liquor. "I thought I was getting over all of this stuff. Guess I was wrong."

"Your drinking?"

"Drinking, Maurice, Ray, flashbacks, all of it."

"You've had a slip, Chris, granted, a big one. But you've also made great gains. This is just a temporary setback. Are you going to be okay? I can come over."

"Yeah, I'll be all right. I'm just going to take it easy for a while." They made plans to meet and said their goodbyes.

Chris spent the rest of the day sprawled on his

futon, listening to music and alternating between occasional periods of sleep and being awakened by intrusive dreams. But he calmed himself somewhat with pleasant thoughts of Stephanie and their plans for the evening.

Chris picked up a pizza on the way to Stephanie's condo. The food was hot, the cola was cold, and Stephanie snuggled against him as they watched a romantic movie starring Ryan Gosling. Chris' thoughts, however, kept drifting farther and farther away.

"You didn't hear what I just said, did you?" Stephanie broke into his reverie.

"Uh?" he grunted, brought back to reality. "Sorry, what did you say?"

"It doesn't matter. Chris, what were you thinking about just now?"

He sighed. "I was thinking about that cruise ship we saw at the harbour. You ever have the urge to just pack up and go?"

"Go where?"

"I don't know. That's the point. Just getting lost somewhere. Anywhere but here."

She uncoiled her arms from Chris and sat up. "What's going on for you right now?"

"Nothing's going on." He told himself it wasn't really a lie because he wasn't entirely sure himself what was going through his head.

"Well, if you won't talk with me, please make sure you do with Nathaniel. When's your next appointment?"

"I haven't made it yet, but I will. And yes, I've been talking with him."

"Good. I'm relieved to hear that at least." There was a moment of uneasy silence between them. Finally, Stephanie stifled a yawn. She checked her phone for the time: eleven o'clock. "Why don't we go to bed?"

"I'd like to stay over, Stephanie, you know that. But I don't want to wake you up in the middle of the night again. I should probably go home." He started to get up.

"Are you sure?" She sounded disheartened.

Chris grudgingly nodded. "I'm sorry for bailing again." He tried to lighten the moment. "Why don't you finish watching the movie? I know you've been waiting for a scene where your fantasy love interest takes off his shirt." Smiling, he leaned down and lightly kissed her forehead.

"I'd have settled for you tonight." She smiled back at him. "Drive safe. I love you."

"I love you, too."

NINETEEN

Arriving at work the next morning feeling lethargic, Chris couldn't concentrate on even the most mundane activities. He wished he'd called in sick. His only hope was to throw himself deeper into his work and somehow fight through his malaise.

He walked onto Alpha Unit and, after some chit-chat with staff, approached Dr. Stevenson in the nursing station. She started to give him a hard time about how bad he looked, but he headed her off by asking for an update on Marvin's assessment.

She knew what he was doing but cut him some slack. "My report is pretty straightforward. I'll be recommending that Marvin is unfit to stand trial. He's not able to describe the rules of the court or the role of the judge or the Crown. I've talked with his lawyer, and she hasn't been able to get any instruction from him. So it's very likely he'll be found unfit."

Dr. Stevenson went on, saying she'd be asking for a treatment order, to give more time to develop a plan with Marvin. She'd also asked Occupational Therapy to complete a functional assessment of Marvin's Activities of Daily Living, and she was waiting on the neuro-psych assessment from Psychology.

"Any luck connecting with Marvin's family?" she asked Chris.

"No. Just the one call." He didn't mention he'd driven by the addresses Marvin had given him. "I'll keep trying."

On the way to his office, Chris dropped in on Gerald, hoping for a friendly distraction.

"I hope you feel better than you look," his friend joshed, "because you look like you just stepped off *The Walking Dead* set."

Chris ignored the comment. "What's going on with you?"

"Apparently nothing as exciting as you. Did you know Lucy Chen from the *Tribune* called me?"

Chris shook his head.

"She found out I was assigned to Ray Owens when he was here. She had a bunch of questions about him, and about you."

"What kind of questions?"

"Don't know. We didn't get that far. I told her I couldn't comment on the case and directed her to

Communications. But I thought you'd want to know she hasn't forgotten about you."

"Lucky me."

"She's not the only one."

"What do you mean?"

"I was listening to CBC Radio a few minutes ago. They reported Ray's got Phillip Bernum now as his lawyer."

"No! You're kidding, right?" As usual, the simple mention of Ray's name tied Chris' stomach in a knot. He was equally dismayed to hear that Ray's lawyer was Phillip Bernum, widely known as Barnum, as in the Barnum and Bailey Circus, from the lawyer's penchant for going after controversial and high-profile criminal cases and turning them into events. Chris recalled an attempt a few years earlier to have Bernum disbarred for alleged unethical conduct, but in his usual fashion, the lawyer had managed to wriggle his way off the hook.

"Last I heard, Ray was representing himself because he was too good for a lawyer."

"That's narcissism for ya. Well, he's got Bernum now. Bernum announced it himself about an hour ago on Twitter."

"Great. They'll make quite the pair." Chris scowled.

"That was the general opinion on the CBC. Your name came up, too."

"How so?"

"They were talking about the charges against Ray,

and when it came to his attempted murder charge, they did a back story on you. How you found Carrier's body, how you saved Elizabeth, and how you're one of the few witnesses the Crown's got. Sounds like the guys charged with Elizabeth's abduction are refusing to cooperate, despite the threat of even longer jail time. And everyone else is dead: James Carrier, Charles Longville, Dale Goode—that was the hit man's name, right?"

"Yeah, I think so." Chris lowered his head into his hands and rubbed his aching temples.

"Sorry, Chris, I didn't mean to bum you out."

"Don't worry about it."

"Have you been subpoenaed yet?"

Chris shook his head.

"Well, maybe they'll forget about it and you won't end up testifying after all."

"Fat chance of that. It's not going to trial for a while, but they made it clear they want me on the stand."

"That was the other thing Bernum announced this morning on Twitter. He's trying to push back the court date. It's clearly a stalling tactic. Un-friggin-believable!"

"I wouldn't expect anything less from him. Hell, from either of them." Chris was tired of talking about Ray. "Gotta go."

The rest of his day moved at a glacial pace, but Chris did his best to focus on accomplishing what work he could until the day finally came to a close.

TWENTY

Back at his apartment that evening, Chris collapsed onto the futon. Sitting alone in the dark suited his mood. He wondered how long it would take him to get to sleep tonight and how many hours of sleep he'd get before his nightmares woke him up again.

His phone rang and his thoughts turned to Stephanie as he grabbed his cell. It wasn't Stephanie's number on call display.

"Chris? It's Mary."

"Oh, hi." He cleared his throat and tried to sound upbeat for his aunt. "Is everything all right?"

"I'm okay. It's Maurice I'm calling about."

"Yeah, he called me out of the blue on Saturday. What's going on with him?"

There was a brief silence. "Chris, your father's dead."

For a split second, Chris thought he had misheard his aunt. Then the reality slowly started to set in. "What? How?"

"I'm so sorry."

"What was the cause of death?" Saying the words felt bizarre to him.

"We don't know yet, but he wasn't well. And I'm sure his drinking didn't help matters."

"When did he die?" A million questions were running through his head. "How did you find out?"

"One of his neighbours, a friend of mine, was trying to reach him but there was no answer on his phone. He went over to the house, looked through the window, and saw Maurice lying on the floor."

Stuck somewhere between shock and disbelief, Chris didn't know what to say.

"Chris, are you okay?" His aunt's words brought him back to the moment.

"Yeah, I guess. I'm surprised, that's all. I mean, I suppose I shouldn't be."

"I know. He wasn't much of a father to you, but he *was* your father all the same. It's very sad."

Chris felt tears welling up. He tried to push his emotions aside by dealing with practicalities. "Where is he, uh, right now?"

"At the Health Sciences Centre. I've already called and given your name as next of kin. I can help with the funeral arrangements, if you like."

In his shock, he hadn't considered the arrangements that would have to be made. "I'd really appreciate it, Aunt Mary. I wouldn't know where to start."

"Maurice called me a few days ago. He knew he didn't have long. He told me his wishes."

Chris was speechless again. Mary picked up on his silence. "I know this is hard right now. If you want, we can talk later."

"No, that's okay. What did he want?"

She gave a light chuckle. "Quick and easy. Those were his exact words. Typical Maurice. He said he didn't want a long, drawn out affair. He wanted cremation and a small ceremony at the Evergreen Funeral Home. They're good; I've used them before. I'll make some calls."

"Did he say anything else? Anything about me?"

"He wanted your phone number, which I gave him. I hope that was okay."

"Yeah, but we didn't talk long." He didn't have it in him to go into the details; he was ashamed of how badly he'd treated his father.

"Once again, I'm sorry, Chris," his aunt said, jolting him back to the present. "Get some rest. We'll talk tomorrow."

Chris called Stephanie, needing to hear her voice, but got her recording. He left a brief message asking her to call, but went to bed without hearing from her.

Chris couldn't sleep that evening, not with so many unresolved feelings clanging out of control in his head. Long-repressed questions kept surfacing in an imaginary conversation with his father. *Why did you turn your back on me when I was a child? What did I ever do to deserve that? Did it ever occur to you that I grew up thinking I must have done something wrong for you to leave?*

The cold, hard truth was starting to settle in. He would never get the chance to ask his father these questions, would never know the answers. He oscillated between waves of sorrow and waves of guilt for how he'd treated his father when they spoke on Saturday night. Maurice had been reaching out to him, for once giving Chris an opportunity to ask the questions he'd struggled with for most of his life. But he'd rejected his father's offer, turning his back on the man. Chris' final act toward Maurice saw him treating his father the same way he himself had always resented being treated, and the realization left him feeling hollow and unhappy. Worse. He felt he was no different than his father.

TWENTY-ONE

The next morning announced its arrival with sunlight shining through Chris' blinds and birds chirping joyfully outside his window. The new day seemed to signal fresh opportunities, but Chris remained stuck in the quagmire of his previous evening's musings and regrets. He didn't know if he could even get out of bed and face the day.

Nathaniel would probably say he was using denial as a coping mechanism and that this could be helpful in the short term by giving him time to adjust to his father's death. He could visualize Nathaniel sitting calmly in his leather chair, earnestly expounding the importance of accepting the reality of death in order to move on with life.

But Chris wasn't ready to move on. His father's death

forced him to accept several truths, including the fact that the number of his blood relatives was dwindling. All he had left was his daughter, Ann Marie, and for her he was eternally grateful. He made a mental note to call Ann Marie to tell her how much he loved her.

And then he had Ray, a half-brother by blood. A man he hated. His already low mood plummeted.

Stephanie's call distracted him from his funk. He broke the news to her.

"Oh, Chris, I'm so sorry. What can I do to help?"

"Just hearing your voice right now feels good."

"When is the funeral?"

"In a couple days. Aunt Mary is taking care of most of it."

"I'll come over to help."

"That's nice, Stephanie, it really is. But I was thinking of heading to Maurice's house to deal with a few things, get some clothes to take to the funeral home." Saying the words felt surreal. "I have no idea how long I'm going to be, and I know you've got to work."

"I can take the day off."

"I'll be fine. I'll call you when I get back. I love you." His voice cracked on the last word.

Chris composed himself for a few moments before making his next call, to his manager, David Evans. He explained the situation, that he'd need to take a few days from work and that he'd complete the necessary paperwork for requesting leave on compassionate grounds.

Next, Chris called his aunt and was relieved but equally guilt-ridden to learn that she'd been busy since early morning taking care of the funeral arrangements. She told him she'd learned Maurice suffered from long-standing alcohol-related liver disease, cirrhosis, and kidney failure. They worked out who was calling whom to pass on the information about Maurice's passing. It was a short list. He thanked his aunt profusely for her help.

Chris' next call was to Deanna. It took him a minute to recall whether Ann Marie had ever actually met Maurice. He concluded that Deanna had met him once but that Ann Marie had never known her grandfather. He was lamenting this fact when his daughter picked up the phone.

"Hi, Sweetie. I thought you'd be in school today."

"Teachers have a Pro-D day. Me and Mommy are looking at pictures from the aquarium. They're so cool!"

"You'll have to show me them, too." It was refreshing to hear the excitement and enthusiasm in his daughter's voice, compared to what he was about to discuss with her mother. "Can I speak with Mommy?"

Before he had a chance to say anything else, Ann Marie was off, handing the phone to her mother. "Hi, Chris. How are you?"

Chris told her about Maurice.

"I'm so sorry to hear that. How are you doing?"

"I don't know, still in shock, mostly. But I thought

I should tell you and let you know about the service, in case you wanted to go."

"I do, and I'm glad you called. Is there anything I can do to help?" There was a brief pause before she continued. "I could have Ann Marie stay with my mother and come over to help you with some of the arrangements. If you want me to, that is."

He was a little surprised. "That's very nice of you, Dee. Aunt Mary is taking care of most of it, but I appreciate your offer." He thought about his daughter. "I don't think I'll be back in time to see Ann Marie this evening. I feel bad about cancelling on her."

"I'll talk with her, Chris. I'm sure she'll understand. And please let me know if you need my help. I'll be there for the service. And again, I'm really sorry."

"Yeah, me too."

TWENTY-TWO

Chris prepared mentally for the task ahead of him: an hour's drive to Maurice's house. He found it sadly ironic that his father had chosen to settle down in a place called Mission when the last years of his life appeared to exhibit little purpose or objective. He listened to music to lift his spirits.

Home is where the heart is, Chris thought as he entered his father's house, knowing that Maurice's place had been anything but. The shack Chris entered showed no outward signs of welcome. The interior was much the same as it had been the last time he'd walked through the dilapidated structure, with a shabby, dirty, worn carpet littered with empty bottles of Captain Morgan and cans of cola. The smell of stale cigarette smoke permeated the air. Chris' glance gravitated to the centre of the living room, to the tattered recliner that had been moulded by Maurice's body through years of overuse.

He took in a deep breath and slowly exhaled as he remembered his angry words: "The next time I see you will be at your funeral. And I promise you, I won't shed a tear."

His tears fell now.

He reminded himself that he was here for a reason. His aunt had suggested he collect any mementos before the cleaning company she hired cleared the years of accumulated junk from the place. Chris realized recently he'd seen only the living room and kitchen area, and there was nothing of value in those rooms.

He ventured into his father's bedroom where his first glance yielded a similar reaction. He opened a closet door and retrieved pants and a shirt for Maurice's final resting place. Next, Chris opened the drawers of a dresser. It felt strange and intrusive to be looking through a dead man's personal effects.

His eyes caught sight of something sticking out of the third drawer. He opened the drawer and did a double take at what lay before him: piles of newspaper clippings, papers, and assorted paraphernalia loosely stacked together almost to the point of overflowing.

He pulled out the bundles and leafed through them. He recognized articles from the *Tribune* covering the events at Woodland Park featuring Chris. Next, he spotted the birth announcement for Ann Marie, and below that a faded invitation addressed to Maurice to attend Deanna and Chris' wedding. Chris' report cards from school were there alongside first- and second-place ribbons from Sports Day school events.

Chris was stunned. He had no idea that his father had followed events in his life. Quite the opposite: every message Maurice had ever given Chris suggested total indifference. Chris searched further through the collection and saw photographs he'd never seen before: photos of a younger, happier, healthier-looking Maurice smiling at the camera, holding hands with Chris' mother, Fiona.

Below the photos was another pile of newspaper articles showcasing Chris' mother. He recognized many of them, and a wave of sorrow almost overwhelmed him. He'd searched these out as a boy, eager to learn the details of his mother's death at the hands of a hostage-taker. He already knew many of the details. His mother had been a nurse at what was then called the Grace Hospital, before it was torn down to make way for a shopping plaza. An inmate was admitted for treatment for suspected heart complications; Chris' mother was the treating nurse. The man took her hostage and killed her.

Looking at the clippings now, Chris was transported back to those days and his desperate search for answers to his mother's murder. The answers had never come.

In his father's room now, Chris realized he was still looking for answers. Why had his father gone to all the effort of collecting these articles about Chris and his mother when he'd always given the appearance that they didn't matter to him?

Chris was struck by the irony that he was learning more about his father now through the man's death. The thought made him curious to know who Maurice was when he was alive.

Finally it was time to leave. Holding the clippings and photos together in a box, Chris took one last look inside his father's house. *Home is where the heart is.* He wondered what had happened to his father's heart to make Maurice the shell of a man he turned out to be.

There was only one person who could possibly know: Aunt Mary.

TWENTY-THREE

After locking up his father's house, Chris called his aunt. She was happy to hear from him and even happier that he was on his way for a visit.

A short time later, he parked his truck in front of her home. She greeted him, took Maurice's clothes, and whisked Chris into her living room. "I didn't know you were coming, so I didn't have time to bake." Mary placed a ham and cheese sandwich, and a selection of fudge brownies—Chris' favourite—on a side table. "I took these out of the freezer right after you called. If they're too cold, let me know and I'll warm them up."

After finishing the sandwich, Chris took one bite of a brownie, then another. "They're great. I have to swing by here more often." He felt guilty now that he didn't make more of an effort to keep in touch with his aunt beyond the occasional phone call.

As if reading his thoughts, Mary reassured him, "You're always welcome, you know that."

They sat on couches slightly across from each other. The living room was impeccably furnished, a stark contrast to the place Chris had just left. He glanced at a painting hanging over a piano, a beautiful nature scene of a stream meandering through a green meadow. His aunt was a gifted painter, and he realized this was from a collection of her own works. He hadn't noticed this one during his last visit.

"How are you doing, Chris?" His aunt's question brought him back to reality.

"Uh ... okay, I guess, under the circumstances. Thanks for all your help. I'd be completely lost if it wasn't for you."

"It's what family is for." She hadn't finished the last word before a tear rolled down the side of her face. "You've had a pretty tough go when it comes to family, I'm sad to say."

A tear escaped Chris' control. He felt it glide down his cheek, tasted its salt as it found its way onto his lip. A lump formed in his throat. He tried to regain control by focussing on practical matters. "I took a few things from his place."

"I'm glad you could find anything through that mess, from the way it was described to me." She shook her head in mild disgust. "Oh, Maurice." She stared off.

Chris wasn't sure where to begin with his questions, and the longer he thought about what approach to take, the harder it became for him to start. Finally, he blurted out, "I found pictures of him with Mom. I'd never seen them together in one before." Reaching into his jacket pocket, he pulled out the picture he had collected and gave it to his aunt.

She looked at it and smiled. "They look so young, don't they?" She stared at it a little longer, as if remembering a better time, before handing it back to Chris.

"I've always wondered what she saw in him," he said. "This picture is the closest I've come to maybe understanding. They look so happy together."

"There was a time when they were." She smiled wistfully. "Your father could be charming. Mischievous and charming at the same time." She paused a moment. "I saw the mischief in his eyes. Your mother, she saw the charm. I think a part of her was drawn to that mischief. She had a kind heart, always looking for the goodness in people. I guess she saw something good in your father."

She looked away from Chris.

"What happened?"

She gave him a look that said *Do you really want to know?* "Maurice liked to gamble. Your mother knew that when she met him. At first, it wasn't a problem. She thought she could change him. But it got worse. He'd gamble away his wages, then wouldn't show up for work at all. Your mother and I would go looking and find him at the casino. He couldn't stop, and I knew he wouldn't stop. I told your mother she should leave him. As hard as it would be for her, I told her there was no other way." She looked at Chris' plate. "Would you like some more brownies? How about a drink? I've got cola."

"No, thanks, I'm fine. So, what happened?"

His aunt gave him a sad smile. "You're what happened. After she became pregnant, your mother gave Maurice an ultimatum: stop gambling or she was leaving." She drew a heavy breath. "It worked for a while. But it was only a matter of time before everything got worse. He was gone longer, spending more money. Money he didn't have, money *they* didn't have. One night, he showed up here begging me for money. I turned him away, told him I wasn't going to enable his gambling. Things got more and more out of control. And then it was over." She looked off in the distance.

"What was over?"

She shivered and hesitated before slowly looking into Chris' eyes. "That part of his life. When your mother died."

"Yes?" He leaned eagerly toward her, waiting for her to continue. "I know Stan Edwards killed my mother. What else is there?" He had a feeling that there was more to know, more that his aunt knew, more that he, too, needed to know.

Tears flowed down Mary's cheeks. "Your father ... your father knew Stan."

"What? I don't understand."

She dabbed at her eyes. "Maurice barged into my house a few nights after your mother's murder. He was so drunk, I couldn't make out what he was saying at first. He blamed me for Fiona's death, said she'd still be alive if I'd loaned him the money. And ..." She paused, then said in a rush, "And then he told me about Stan. How he owed Stan money, how Stan threatened him if he didn't pay."

Chris couldn't believe what he was hearing. "What happened?"

She took a few deep breaths before continuing. "I don't know the details, but I gather Maurice was scared enough that he went to the police and told them about Stan's illegal activities, loan sharking and the like. He couldn't have known what was going to happen. And neither could I."

She took a moment to collect herself. "Stan was arrested and went to jail. A week later, my sister was dead. Oh, Chris, I'm so sorry." She started sobbing uncontrollably. Chris approached his aunt and put his arms around her. "I love you, Aunt Mary. We don't have to talk about this anymore if you don't want to."

"No, it's okay. You can ask me whatever you want."

Chris was dumbfounded. In every article he'd read, his mother's murder had never been depicted as anything other than a tragic act of random violence. His head was thumping. He felt overcome by this new information, but it still left him with questions.

"How come this was never in the news? Why didn't you tell me?" He looked at Mary with surprise.

Her damp tissue was in shreds. "I don't know why it wasn't reported. Part of me prayed all these years that it wasn't true. I prayed that it was Maurice's drunken rambling, that none of it happened the way he said."

"But why didn't *you* tell me what he'd said?"

She spoke without looking at him. "After Fiona's death, Maurice went out of control. He traded one vice for another. I never saw or heard of him stepping a foot inside a casino again, but he became a horrible drunk. He cut everyone out of his life, including you. I guess he felt responsible for her death. That's one thing we shared. I've lived with this guilt all these years, Chris. I've been afraid to tell you."

"But why?"

"At first, I held out hope your father would re-enter your life. I didn't tell you because I was afraid that if you knew the truth, you'd never forgive him. Or me." She looked at him now with pleading eyes.

"So why are you telling me now?"

"Last week, your father showed up at my door. It was the first time in years we'd seen each other. He knew he was dying, Chris. He said he had a few things to straighten out before ..."

She stopped herself, then started again. "He said he had to tell me the truth about Fiona's death, about Stan. He didn't remember telling me all those years ago when he was drunk. The story was the same. He also wanted you to know, which is why he asked for your number. You deserve to know. All these years, I've known you should know."

Chris felt as though a two-by-four had whacked him on his head. Another question popped up that he felt compelled to ask. "What about Ray? Did you know that my father had another child?"

"No. I didn't know that until you told me a few months ago. I swear."

"Do you think my mother knew?"

She shook her head. "I'm sure if she'd known, she'd have told me."

Chris' head was spinning, overcome by a myriad of conflicting emotions. He'd always loved his aunt, and he knew she'd loved him ever since she took him in as a young boy. But now he felt he'd been kept in the dark about much of his mother's life. His aunt had known for years that his mother's death was not a random act, that it was a planned, deliberate act of revenge.

At this point, he didn't know what difference this knowledge made, but it still hurt. He had to get out of there.

Chris said something about having to hit the road before it got too late. He thanked his aunt for the brownies and made a quick retreat.

His drive home was going to be long and lonely, and he needed to hear a familiar voice, but his call to Stephanie went straight to voicemail. Needing the sound of human voices, he switched on the radio.

Low-lying fog made visibility poor on long stretches of Highway 1, and Chris was forced to drive with his fog lights on when there were no oncoming vehicles. It wasn't much better after he took the last exit to lead him home. As he neared his building, the vehicle behind him suddenly put on its high beams. The intense glare distracted Chris. As he adjusted his mirror to avoid the glare, he saw that the large vehicle was closing its distance on his truck. Cursing to himself, he checked his rear-view mirror a second time to get a better look at the inept driver. He wasn't sure but it looked like a black Expedition.

"What the hell do you want from me?" he shouted. He slammed on his brakes and came to a sudden stop in the middle of the road. The tires on the black SUV screeched wildly to avoid a collision, and the driver, hidden behind tinted windows, blasted the horn in protest before pulling a one-eighty and racing away.

Chris pulled over to the side of the road, turned off the ignition, and waited for his heart to stop pounding. He was furious and embarrassed in equal measure that his panicked actions had almost caused an accident. When he finally came to his senses, he resumed his slow drive home.

It was after ten when he arrived at his apartment. He phoned Stephanie to report that he was home and heading straight to bed. He turned in for the night, but wasn't counting on getting much sleep.

TWENTY-FOUR

Chris felt no more rested the next morning. After being terrorized by yet another nightmare, he hadn't been able to get back to sleep for several hours. He didn't have the energy to record the nightmare in his dream diary and figured it didn't matter because this was one dream he wasn't going to forget. He'd be discussing it with Nathaniel soon enough.

A phone call interrupted his thoughts. Reaching for the phone, he realized he also had messages waiting. The caller identified himself as the warden at the West Coast Correctional Centre. Chris' breathing quickened, his heart pulsing. *Why was the warden calling him? Was Stephanie okay? Or was it Ray?*

"I'm sorry to interrupt your morning, Mr. Ryder. Please accept my condolences on the loss of your father."

"Thanks," Chris said suspiciously. "Is something wrong?"

"Yes, unfortunately, and that's why I'm calling.

Mr. Ray Owens has been granted permission from Correctional Service Canada to attend his, uh, your father's funeral."

It took Chris a moment to process the information before he exploded in a rage. "You've got to be joking!"

"I'm afraid not," the man replied in a tone more reserved than Chris'. "I understand this is coming to you as a surprise, and an unwelcome one at that. I'm also aware of the history between yourself and Mr. Owens. If it were solely up to me, we wouldn't be having this conversation. I would have rejected the request and been done with it. This is a staffing and logistical problem that I would much sooner not have to deal with."

"So what's the problem?"

"The problem ..." The warden stopped as if searching for a diplomatic way to express himself. "The problem is that Mr. Owens' lawyer, Mr. Bernum, is exerting an enormous amount of pressure on us to accommodate his client's request on legal and compassionate grounds."

"Compassionate grounds! Ray doesn't have a compassionate bone in his miserable body. He doesn't give a damn about my father's death. He didn't even know the man. Compassion? Get real!"

"I don't disagree with you. However, Mr. Bernum is using part of that very rationale to force the request through the Correctional Service of Canada as a temporary absence. He's arguing that Mr. Owens never had a chance to meet his father while he was alive and therefore deserves an opportunity to pay his respects at the funeral service."

"How did Ray even find out?"

"That I don't know, Mr. Ryder. I suspect his lawyer may have had a hand in it. I trust you're familiar with Mr. Bernum."

Chris was speechless. He would have hoped common sense and decency would prevail in a situation like this. But Ray had Bernum as his lawyer, so common sense and decency were thrown out the window. Ray's intention of making a mockery of the justice system had sunk to a new low.

"Let the circus begin," he muttered.

"What was that, Mr. Ryder?"

"Nothing. Is there anything, anything at all, I can do to stop this?" he said helplessly.

"I'm afraid not. This lawyer seems to have found a sympathetic ear at a higher pay grade than mine."

"So what happens now?"

"Well, first, I want you to know that we'll take every precaution to ensure that Mr. Owens conducts himself in a respectful manner and that his behaviour doesn't become a distraction for the other attendees, yourself included."

"His very presence is going to be a distraction," Chris responded angrily. He took a few deep breaths. "Sorry, I don't mean to shoot the messenger. It's just that this whole thing sounds like a gong show, and that's exactly what Ray wants it to be."

"I understand, Mr. Ryder. What I can assure you is that he'll be shackled and cuffed the whole time. And I will personally ensure the two guards escorting him are fully briefed about the situation."

"Thanks," Chris said unenthusiastically. He confirmed the details of the service with the warden and hung up.

It occurred to him that his entire life was becoming one big nightmare, one that he fervently hoped would soon end.

He needed a run. He put on his gear, grabbed his iPod, and stepped outside into the brisk air. U2 blasted through his headphones as he took to the street. He was running in his neighbourhood out of necessity rather than preference. His favourite running spot had been Woodland Park and he'd yet to find a suitable substitute.

There had been a time when running had provided clarity of thought and helped Chris deal with life's challenges. But the events at Woodland Park had now made the very act of running a challenge, just as they had affected so many other aspects of his life. Still, he gritted his teeth in silent fury and pushed through his initial anxiety. He was rewarded with the massive physical release he'd been desperately looking for.

Back at his apartment, he started checking his voicemail. Various friends and colleagues from IFP had called to express their condolences, and most offered to attend the funeral service for support. Chris wasn't ready to return their calls just yet. He also had a message from Lucy Chen at the *Tribune*. He didn't bother listening to that one. Instead, he phoned Stephanie, briefed her on his call from the warden, and made plans to meet for coffee at a Starbucks near his place after she got off work. Then he left a message with Nathaniel, letting him know they'd have to re-schedule their appointment.

In the meantime, he could make the final prepa-rations for his father's funeral. That part of the afternoon felt surreal to him, especially as he tried to reflect on his father's life, only to realize how little he knew about the man. His sadness was matched by the confused feelings he felt for his aunt as well as by his anger toward Ray. He wasn't sure how he was going to react when he saw either of them at the service.

Upon spotting Stephanie at the coffee shop, he gave her an extended kiss and a warm hug. "You have no idea how much I've missed you."

"I've missed you, too."

After ordering a latte for her and a strong dark roast for him, he updated her on his eventful past few days. Stephanie provided a supportive ear and a com-forting shoulder for him to lean on. "We'll get through this, Chris."

As he listened to Stephanie and watched as her eyes crinkled when she smiled, Chris started to feel desire for her simmering inside him. And from the way Stephanie's leg casually caressed his, he realized she had similar feelings. Leaving most of their drinks behind, they raced to Chris' apartment and made love. Afterwards, they lay silently in each other's arms.

"You need a plant in here," Stephanie finally said with a smile as she looked around the lifeless apartment.

"That's the first thing that comes to your mind?" he responded, pretending to be hurt.

"It's such a guy's place. Futon, TV, fridge," she continued, playfully ignoring him. "I'll bet there's nothing in your fridge except leftover pizza and beer."

"I'd be lucky if I had pizza. I admit, though, your place is nicer."

"It's tidier, too." She looked around. "Your futon doesn't even sleep two, at least not comfortably."

"You weren't complaining a few minutes ago."

"We weren't sleeping," she said with a grin. "Guess I'll be sleeping in my own bed tonight."

"Is that a hint?" He suspected she was talking about them getting a place together.

"I've been thinking about what you said."

"And?"

"And ... I'm still thinking. I agree, though, I don't want to rush things."

Chris pulled her closer. "We can take however long we need."

They dressed, ordered Chinese food, and spent the remainder of the evening binge-watching a new series on Netflix, huddled in each other's arms.

Stephanie broke their reverie. "When do you want to meet up tomorrow?"

Thinking about the funeral opened a pit in Chris' stomach. "Noon. I'll call before heading over," he said solemnly.

Stephanie picked up on his changed mood. "Are you going to be okay tonight? I can stay and keep you company."

"I'll be fine. You're welcome to stay. Even though my futon doesn't compare to your bed."

"I do like my bed," she said, kissing his forehead. "All right, I'll see you tomorrow. We'll get through it together."

He nodded and walked Stephanie to her car.

TWENTY-FIVE

Chris awoke the next morning to a text from Gerald alerting him to a piece in the day's *Tribune*. He scrolled through the site on his smartphone until he saw the headline: *Accused Killer to Attend Father's Funeral*. His shock soon gave way to anger as he read the article by Lucy Chen.

> The *Vancouver Tribune* has learned that Ray Owens has received Temporary Absence permission from the Correctional Service of Canada to attend the funeral of his father.
>
> The *Tribune* was contacted by Mr. Owens himself, who indicated that he will be in attendance at today's ceremony at Evergreen Funeral Home in Vancouver as Maurice Ryder is laid to rest.
>
> Ray Owens is currently in custody awaiting trial on several charges including two counts of

murder and one count of attempted murder, stemming from an incident at Woodland Park earlier this year.

Maurice Ryder leaves behind another son, Chris Ryder.

Neither Chris Ryder nor Correctional Service Canada could be reached for comment.

Ray Owens' lawyer, Phillip Bernum, provided the following statement: "This great country of ours presumes that its citizens are innocent until proven guilty. Through that lens, my client, Mr. Owens, is innocent, and as such, he has every right to attend the service for his recently departed father. Mr. Owens has asked for privacy during his time of mourning and will not be commenting further at this time."

Chris closed the site in disgust.

He wasn't surprised by Ray's antics, but he was irked at the man's brazen and insensitive act of calling the paper to inform them about the funeral and its location, and then having the audacity to ask for privacy. He now knew why Chen had left him a message the day before.

The morning had started with a light mist, but soon rain was falling, accentuating the gloominess of the day. Just before noon, Chris picked up Stephanie, who kept the conversation light as they made their way to Evergreen Funeral Home.

After parking the truck, Chris and Stephanie walked hand in hand toward the people congregated outside the building. He solemnly acknowledged

Brandon and other friends, as well as Dr. Stevenson, Gerald, and Horace from IFP.

Chris walked over to Deanna, who gave him a light hug. They'd decided earlier that Ann Marie wouldn't attend the service; instead, she was spending the day with Deanna's mother. Deanna and Stephanie exchanged awkward pleasantries while Chris looked around for Aunt Mary. She was standing next to the minister, and she waved when she spotted Chris.

Chris was about to go over to greet her when he was distracted by the appearance of Ray escorted by two guards. An intense feeling of terror immediately overcame him. Stephanie took his hand firmly in hers and whispered in his ear. "It's going to be okay. You're with family and friends who love you. Ray is nobody. Forget about him." His panic gradually subsided.

Ray's hands were cuffed and his feet shackled. Wearing an orange correctional jumpsuit, he stood out among the somber blacks and greys of the other mourners. Chris recalled the warden saying that Ray would be given the opportunity to wear more appropriate clothing given the circumstances; he figured that wearing correctional apparel was another example of Ray choosing to make a spectacle.

The minister commenced the ceremony with a prayer. She said a few things about Maurice and the biblical view of death before introducing Chris' aunt. Mary approached the podium and gave a touching eulogy, highlighting the charming characteristics of the younger Maurice her sister had loved so many years before. She then announced that Maurice's son, Chris, had a few things to say.

Chris approached the podium, aware that his hands were trembling, making the paper holding his prepared speech appear to vibrate. He cleared his throat and began.

"The truth is, I never really knew my father. He, along with my mother, has always been a mystery to me. I've learned a few things in the brief time since his passing. I think, in his own way, he loved me. I wish I'd known that. And I wish I'd had a chance to get to know him —" Chris struggled to get the last word out. Tears filled his eyes, and a large lump in his throat prevented him from saying anything else. He stared blankly at his prepared speech, paralyzed. Stephanie approached the podium and stood beside Chris, taking his hand in hers. Touched by her loving act of support, Chris summoned the resolve to finish his speech. They walked back to their seats together. People wiped tears from their eyes, and the sound of sniffling filled the room.

As the ceremony drew to a close, the minister began a final prayer.

"Hey, I got a few words to say," Ray interrupted. He smiled at the two guards as though issuing a challenge. The guards exchanged a look that appeared to be a mixture of confusion, surprise, and frustration, then escorted Ray to the podium. The clanking of shackles was impossible to ignore.

Ray cleared his throat in dramatic fashion before starting to speak. "Like my dear brother said, I too never knew my father. But you won't see me up here bawling like a baby," he said, breaking into laughter. He was the only one laughing. "I like to think I am the man I am today because of Maurice."

He looked at Chris with his all-too-familiar smirk. "I take great comfort being here today with all of you, the family I never knew I had. We need to cherish these moments and hold our loved ones close because no one knows what tomorrow brings. Life can be cruel. Lives can be struck down in an instant. And we're left asking ourselves, 'Why did this happen?' Rest in peace, Maurice. May you find company soon." He looked daggers at Chris.

Chris could feel his blood boiling. He was furious at Ray and his obvious threat.

The minister, appearing visibly frazzled, resumed her final prayer. The ceremony ended, and Chris stood to receive condolences from his friends.

As Ray was being escorted out of the building back to the guards' vehicle, he shouted, "I'm sorry I didn't get a chance to meet your daughter, Ryder." He waited until he had Chris' attention before adding, "Maybe next time."

"Don't respond, Chris. He's just trying to get a rise out of you," Stephanie whispered.

Chris let the waves of fury roll over him. "Class

act, isn't he?" Chris finally said as his heart rate returned to normal.

As his friends departed, his family congregated. Chris hesitated briefly when his Aunt Mary was in front of him. He was still processing her recent disclosure, but the emotion of the day took over and tears spilled from his eyes as he embraced her tightly.

"I'm so sorry, Chris," she said softly in his ear. Then, "You did the right thing not reacting to that monster."

"Thank you," he whispered back. "I love you."

Chris introduced Stephanie to his aunt, then walked over to Deanna to say goodbye.

Chris drove Stephanie to her condo before heading back to his apartment. He put on some music and waited for exhaustion to force him to sleep.

TWENTY-SIX

Although he wasn't feeling up to it, Chris decided to return to work the next morning. Horace approached Chris as he checked in at the reception desk. "How are you doing?"

"Okay, considering."

"Ray Owens made quite the scene yesterday."

"Couldn't pass up an opportunity to make it all about him."

"Well, here's something that might cheer you up. I've got an extra ticket for the Canucks game on Sunday. I'll be meeting up with Gerald and a few other guys. Interested?"

Chris wasn't, and normally he'd come up with some excuse and politely decline. But he didn't have it in him to say no today and stamp out the look of excitement on Horace's face. Besides, maybe seeing a playoff game would shake him from his current funk.

"Sure. But I'm not painting my face, holding up a sign, or whatever goofy thing you usually do," he joshed.

"Funny guy. The least you can do, then, is wear a jersey. Think you can handle that?"

"I'm sure I've got one stored away somewhere that I can dust off. How much do I owe you for the ticket?"

"Don't worry about it. We can settle that later. Besides, I know where you work."

They discussed the details of when and where they'd meet at the arena.

Chris headed to his office. He hadn't been there five minutes before Gerald appeared at his door. "How're you doing?" He walked into the room and perched on the edge of the desk.

"All right, I guess."

"How was it, uh, with Ray being there?"

"About what I'd expected. He went out of his way to make an ass of himself, didn't he?"

"I read the statement from Bernum. The two of them managed to create a shitstorm, but people are seeing right through it. It was one of the most talked-about segments on the Nick Stromme show this morning. Callers have been unanimous that Ray had no business attending the funeral. I can only imagine what that was like for you."

Chris nodded. "How have things been around here?"

"Same old, same old. Everyone is complaining about the day-leave thing, and no one's telling us when it'll end."

"I'm sorry I wasn't around. I'm sure you ended up dealing with a bunch of calls about my patients."

"No problem, we had it covered."

"I hear you're going to the Canucks game. Horace is selling me his extra ticket."

"Yeah, he told me he was gonna ask you. That's great. The first beer's on me, and maybe even the second. Depends on whether the Canucks are winning or losing," Gerald joked.

Chris glanced at his phone. The flashing red light told him he had messages waiting. Gerald picked up on the cue. "I'll let you get caught up. Talk later."

Chris spent the rest of the morning dealing with the work he'd missed the last few days. Returning phone calls, seeing a newly admitted remand patient, and starting a referral to a mental-health boarding home in Vancouver for another patient. In preparation for the afternoon meeting about Marvin, he followed up his previous calls to Community Living Society about the referral he'd initiated.

He worked through lunch. In the early afternoon, he ventured onto Alpha Unit and met Dr. Stevenson in the nursing station.

As usual, the unit was humming with activity. A patient was being prepared to attend court transported by the BC Sheriff's Department. The phones were ringing constantly, and members from two treatment teams had assembled in the nursing station while waiting for their respective meetings to start.

All activity came to a brief but sudden halt when Chris entered the nursing station. He noticed the day-old newspaper on the counter bearing the inflammatory headline.

Dr. Stevenson broke the silence. "How are you doing, Chris?"

"Good. Thanks for asking." Uncomfortable at being the centre of attention, Chris attempted to divert the focus. "How's Marvin?"

Dr. Stevenson smiled. "Let's grab a room so we can talk. Marvin will be joining us later."

Alex gave Chris an update on Marvin. "He's had a few unsettled moments. There was one day when he didn't get a paper —"

"Oh, I'm so sorry," Chris interrupted, his face flushed with embarrassment. "I was off, and it completely skipped my mind to bring a copy down."

"No, no, it's fine. He has his own copy of the *Tribune* now, and for some reason, the delivery was delayed. But he came to me with a note, just like we asked him. He dealt with it all right." Alex continued with his update on Marvin.

"His court date's coming up," Dr. Stevenson reported, "but he won't be discharged. I'm going to certify him under the Mental Health Act. I've talked with his lawyer, and we're looking to have Marvin attend by video from here rather than in person in Hope. I've recommended he's unfit to stand trial. Hopefully, we'll get the treatment order to give us more time to see if we can help him, but the reality is that he may never be fit enough to stand trial."

"What then?" Alex asked.

"Well, with any luck our assessments will get him the help he needs," she said, filing through Marvin's chart. "I see the Occupational Therapy functional assessment has been done." She skimmed through the report outlining Marvin's low performance with money management and home health and safety, then read the recommendation aloud. "'Low scores in our assessment suggests Mr. Goodwin doesn't have the necessary skills to safely live independently or semi-independently in the community. Mr. Goodwin would function optimally in a fully supported living environment where he has assistance with activities of daily living such as cooking and home management.'" Dr. Stevenson continued. "Psychology also finished the neuro-psych testing, which showed significant challenges with language, reasoning, judgement, and problem solving."

"I faxed it to CLS," Chris said. "They're still reviewing it to confirm whether he meets their criteria. But even if they agree that he needs a home with specialized care twenty-four/seven, he'll be put on a waitlist for who knows how long."

"So we're stuck with him and he's stuck with us?" Alex asked.

"Where else could he go?" Chris asked rhetorically.

"You're right," said Dr. Stevenson. "Jail is not a practical option, nor an ethical one, for that matter." She looked at Chris. "No word from his family?"

Chris shook his head and made a mental note to drive by the addresses Marvin had given him again to see if he'd have better luck connecting with someone this time.

"If you're ready, I'll go get him." Alex left the room.

Marvin appeared at the door a short while later. "Hi, Marvin, thank you for coming. Please take a seat."

Looking nervous, Marvin took his time entering the room. He appeared hesitant about sitting down.

"It's okay, Marvin, take any seat," Alex encouraged. Marvin sat down, his right hand still clutching the day's newspaper displaying the sports section.

"Are you having a good day, Marvin?" Dr. Stevenson asked.

"Good day," the young man repeated, nodding his head slightly. Then, turning to look at Chris, he said, "Home."

Chris gave him a smile. "We were talking about that just before you came in. We want you to go home, but we need to find out what the best home will be for you. For example, if you don't live with your brother, we'll help you find another home, one where there are people who can help you with your meals and things like that. Would that be okay?"

Unsurprisingly, Marvin's response was limited to "Home." Dr. Stevenson fared no better when she tried asking him a few questions. Finally, Marvin stood up, signalling that he wanted to leave.

Chris thought of something. "I know you like to read the stats on the Canucks, Marvin. Do you like watching them on TV?" There was no response. "If you do, I'm sure you could watch when they play their next game. I'm actually going to that game and I was thinking of buying a program. It will have information about each of the players, maybe even some stats on them. Would you be interested in reading it?"

"Reading."

Chris could swear he saw the glimmer of a smile on the young man's face. "All right, I'll bring it in. See you soon."

Alex stood up to escort Marvin back to his room. He looked at Chris. "Good to see you back. Enjoy the game."

When they were alone, Dr. Stevenson echoed Alex's sentiment. "How are you holding up?"

"As well as can be expected."

She paused. Chris knew she was waiting for a more detailed response from him, but he said nothing, so she continued. "What was it like seeing Ray? The truth," she added with a smile.

Chris wasn't feeling ready to talk about his father

or Ray, but Marilyn Stevenson was more than a colleague. She was a friend, a friend who was reaching out to support another friend. He took a deep breath and tried to summarize the multitude of emotions banging away in his mind. "Yesterday was rough. I was sad, angry ... you name it." He shrugged. "But there's not much I could do about any of it."

Marilyn took a moment to respond. "I see he's got Phillip Bernum representing him. I heard Bernum's been shopping around for a psychiatrist to conduct another NCR assessment on Ray."

"You don't think he could be found not criminally responsible, do you?"

"I certainly saw no supporting evidence when I conducted my assessment with him. Can you imagine the chaos he'd create if he was admitted here again?"

"I can. That's the problem," Chris said, trying to shake the thought from his mind.

Marilyn picked up on his reaction. "Are you still seeing a counsellor?" Chris nodded but said nothing, so she changed the topic. "And how are things between you and Stephanie?"

"Good," he said, fidgeting in his chair. He knew Marilyn meant well, but he was feeling too mentally and physically tired to engage in a frank conversation about his personal life, especially when he feared it was unravelling around him.

"Listen, Chris, I know I said a few things a few months back about you and Stephanie seeing each other. Perhaps I was out of line back then. I was worried about you rushing into a relationship so soon after your separation and what happened to you at Woodland Park. But these past couple of months, you've looked happier, and that's been good to see. I wish the best for you both."

"Thanks, Marilyn."

Marilyn took her time before continuing. "I'm sure you know how hard it is for caregivers to be in the position of needing to get care for themselves. But Chris, if you're not feeling ready to be back at work—"

"I'll be fine, Marilyn, really. But I appreciate your concern. I'd better get going. Have a good afternoon."

He stood and left the unit.

TWENTY-SEVEN

Next, Chris went to see his patient Paul on Beta Unit. Staff there gave him a similar reception as that on Alpha. Some expressed condolences over his father's passing while others couldn't resist asking about Chris' recently disclosed biological connection to Ray. All were interested, however, in hearing his reaction to Ray being at his father's funeral service. He didn't want to appear rude, so he did his best to give quick, well-rehearsed responses to their questions before asking to see Paul.

"How long do you think you'll be with Paul? We're going to the airing court in fifteen minutes." Chris knew the unit would normally go to the gymnasium as a group, but with the day's sun and warm temperature, the option of going to the airing court was too good to pass up. Though fenced for security, the courtyard boasted a large grassy area where patients, and occasionally staff, played volleyball and soccer in the summer, as well as a paved area for basketball.

"We'll be done by then," Chris said.

A healthcare worker named Craig went to get Paul from his room.

When the young man arrived, they both moved to an interview room for privacy.

Chris started by explaining why he'd missed their last team meeting.

"I read about it in the paper. Sorry about your father."

"Yeah, me too." From the way Paul looked at him, Chris got the impression that he had more to say about the matter. He guessed it probably had to do with him and Ray being related, but he wasn't ready to discuss that quite yet. To head off further questions about Ray, he said, "I had a message from your mother thanking me for coordinating her visit with you. She said it went well. What did you think?"

"It was really good seeing her again," Paul said with a grin.

"That's great. The timing was unfortunate with the hold on day passes, but hopefully the next time she visits, you'll be able to have one outside of this place."

Paul was silent for a moment. "Uh, do you know when those passes are gonna start again? The supervisor at the clubhouse is offering me more hours in the communications department but they're on days that the staff don't take us, so I'd need to have a pass to go on my own."

Chris shook his head. "They're still doing the review. I hope it'll be done soon." He saw the disappointed look on Paul's face. "I'll tell you what. I'll look into whether our staff can take you for an extra day. Would that help?" Paul nodded with excitement. "You're leaving quite a good impression on the other members at the clubhouse. Keep up the good work. Who knows where it could lead?"

"Yeah, I know. Thanks."

"Have a good time outside. It's a nice day to be out."

They walked back to the dining area where a collection of patients and staff had gathered in preparation to going to the airing court. Chris returned to his office.

Chris had no sooner reached his office when he received a call from Alex on Alpha Unit.

"Phillip Bernum is waiting in reception. Says he has an appointment with Marvin. Is that true?"

"No. Bernum isn't Marvin's lawyer!"

"Do you want me to tell Security to turn him away?"

"That's okay, I'll deal with it."

Chris raced down to reception.

"Ah, Mr. Ryder," Bernum said with an ingratiating smile. He stood up and stretched out his hand in an overly dramatic fashion. "Let me introduce myself. I'm —"

"I know who you are." Chris ignored the outstretched hand. "You're not Marvin's lawyer."

Bernum feigned surprise at Chris' reaction. "How astute of you. It just so happens that Mr. Goodwin's lawyer was called away this afternoon, and I offered to drop in to see the poor young man as a professional courtesy. I like to think of my colleagues as extended family who would reciprocate the favour under similar circumstances."

A look of false sympathy replaced the feigned surprise. "Speaking of family, please accept my condolences on the loss of your father. Losing loved ones can leave such a devastating void in our lives. I know my client, Mr. Owens, has been deeply affected by his loss. But onward and upward, I always say." A smile returned to his face.

Chris wasn't buying Bernum's story that his sudden presence at IFP was an act of altruism. And he was curious to know more.

"I'll call Marvin's lawyer to sort this out."

"That won't be necessary. I just wanted to make sure the young man had legal representation, and you've confirmed that for me."

The man reached out his hand once again to Chris, and again Chris declined.

"I understand how unpleasant this all must be for you, Mr. Ryder. I wish I could say that Mr. Owens' trial, if and when it occurs, will be a more pleasant experience, but sadly, I can't. As with any murder trial, the stakes are high, and I'll be aggressively defending my client to the fullest extent." He paused for a moment before continuing. "But there's no reason we can't be civil with each other throughout the proceedings."

"I can think of a reason."

Bernum chuckled. "Ray Owens. Well, yes, indeed. Be that as it may, I wish you well." And with that, he smiled slyly and walked out of the building.

Chris was finding it hard to contain his anger. He'd clenched his teeth so hard and for so long during his interaction with Bernum that his jaw ached. He marched back to his office and immediately called Sergeant Ryan. The instant Brandon picked up, Chris started to vent. "You're not going to believe who I just ran into. Phillip Bernum!"

"Where?"

Chris filled Brandon in on his conversation with Bernum. "I knew there was something about Marvin's case that wasn't right, and Bernum just proved it."

"Whoa, Chris, slow down. Couldn't he have been telling the truth about seeing Marvin? He *is* a criminal defence lawyer, after all."

"Come on, Brandon. Do you really think Bernum's the kind of guy who reaches out to do favours? No, he's Ray's lawyer, and now he's asking about Marvin. He's looking for something."

"What he's looking for is publicity. He's an ambulance chaser, Chris. He's probably attracted to the Goodwin case because of its notoriety."

Deflated, Chris was silent for a long moment. "Maybe you're right."

"How are you doing, Chris?"

"Surviving."

"Ray attending the funeral was a pretty low blow. I know how much you hate him, and now to have Bernum fighting in his corner, that's pretty tough."

"Yeah." Chris wasn't interested in talking further about it. "I should let you go." They ended their call.

As Chris was getting ready to leave for the day, David appeared in his doorway. "I came by a few times, to catch up with you, Chris. Busy day?"

"Yeah, it was." He figured David was looking for the paperwork for the time he'd taken as compassionate leave. "I've got the form here. I just need to sign it."

"I didn't come to pick up the form. I wanted to check in and see how you are doing. There's no reason to rush your return. Come back when you're ready."

"Uh-huh."

"*Are* you ready to be back?" David asked bluntly.

"Uh ... yeah," Chris responded, although truthfully, he wasn't so sure.

"Because it won't do anyone any good if you're not."

Chris nodded but said nothing. He was just so tired of all of it. People's questions about him and his father and Ray and the funeral service. All of it.

David continued to look at him, waiting for him to say something, but Chris had no desire to talk further. He respected his manager and knew that he was doing his job diligently in asking his questions. But Chris simply didn't feel ready to discuss how he was doing right now.

"Well, I'll see you tomorrow," David finally said, and left the office.

Five o'clock finally rolled around, and Chris sighed with relief as he closed his office door and left the building. Pulling out of the IFP parking lot, he thought about tonight's session with Nathaniel. He had a couple hours before their rescheduled meeting and considered his options for spending that time.

What he really wanted to do was spend it with Stephanie. Instead, he chose to drive through the two Vancouver neighbourhoods with the addresses Marvin had given him, on the off chance that someone might be home when he showed up. He was tired and hungry, and his mood was becoming increasingly foul. But more than anything, he was determined to understand the connection between Marvin and these addresses.

This evening's excursion went no better than the last one. There was no answer at the door of the first house, and the expanding collection of newspapers and flyers reinforced his suspicion that it was unoccupied. And while there was no indication that the second house had been abandoned, there was no response there when he knocked at the front door. This time, however, he did notice the surveillance camera looking down at him. He glared back at the camera for a long minute, as if daring the owner to make the next move, before he finally looked away. A part of him realized what he was doing was irresponsible, dangerous even, and a clear departure from how he normally behaved. But there was another part of Chris that was starting to surface with increasing frequency, a part of Chris that didn't care.

He walked back to his truck and drove off to his counsellor's office. All the while, he debated whether to share this latest escapade with Nathaniel, because he had enough to worry about and didn't want his poor judgement at work piling on the ever-growing list.

His smartphone beeped. Stephanie had texted "Thinking of you" with a love-heart emoji.

"Love you," he texted back.

TWENTY-EIGHT

Chris had told Nathaniel about his father's death when he called to reschedule their appointment, but a lot had happened since then and, as he told Nathaniel now, he wasn't sure where to start.

"Why don't we start with your father's funeral? How was that for you?"

Despite his attempt to contain his emotions, a tear rolled down Chris' face. He made a feeble attempt to wipe it away; Nathaniel encouraged him to cry and to take as long as he needed. Chris took several deep breaths until he felt ready to talk. "Everyone's asked me the same question about my father: 'How are you doing?' How am I supposed to be doing? I didn't know him well and what I did know I hated. I feel guilty saying that, but it's how I feel. Or, at least, how I used to feel." He took another breath to collect himself. "I don't know why it's affecting me this way."

"Your reaction has surprised you?"

"Yeah." Chris didn't look at Nathaniel.

"Your reaction seems entirely appropriate to me, Chris. Are you familiar with the Stress Scale?"

"Yeah."

"Well, you've experienced several stressors over the last few months: marital separation, personal injury, and now death of a family member. Each one of these can be life-changing events. So, it's not at all surprising that you'd be feeling the way you are right now."

"And Ray was at the funeral."

"I read that in the paper."

"Everyone and their grandma did."

"So how was it for you, seeing Ray?"

"Predictable. My heart started pounding. I went straight into panic-attack mode. Stephanie helped me get through it; I couldn't have done it without her. Would you believe Ray had the gall to threaten my daughter? At a funeral. A funeral he had no business being at in the first place!"

"So you were angry."

"Damn right, I was angry." Chris looked at Nathaniel now. "And scared."

"Tell me about that."

"I'd do anything to protect Ann Marie. It'd kill me if anything happened to her. Or Stephanie or Deanna, for that matter. But I worry whether I can protect them from him. It keeps me up at night."

He shifted in his chair and cleared his throat. "Speaking of which, you asked me to keep a dream diary. I've had some doozies." He opened his diary. "Do you really want to hear them?" he asked, glancing at Nathaniel.

"Absolutely."

"All right ... So, I'm in a truck. I'm a passenger. I don't know who's driving. I guess that's not important. But it's racing down this street, basically a steep hill that I used to live on when I was a kid. I'm in the back seat, and there's someone in the seat next to me but I can't see who it is. I close my eyes and brace myself because I know there's going to be an enormous crash when we hit the brick church at the bottom of the hill. And I'm waiting and waiting. But it doesn't crash. At least, I don't remember it in the dream. The next thing I *do* remember, I'm outside looking in at the truck, and it's hard to make out what it is, or was. Now it's a mangled wreck of metal and I'm staring at it, spitting dirt out of my mouth. Paramedics are trying to get to the driver. I remember thinking to myself, there's no way anyone could survive that crash, so how did I?"

Chris stopped for a moment and looked skeptically at Nathaniel. "Is this the kind of thing you want me to talk about?"

"If it's your dream, then yes. Please go on."

"Okay. The next thing I remember, I'm walking down this street, still spitting dirt out of my mouth, when I come to an intersection. I remember wondering, which way do I cross? I don't know where I'm supposed to go, so I'm just standing there at this intersection and I'm starting to panic because I don't know what to do next. I'm lost. Someone appears out of nowhere and points a finger at a building behind me. I turn my head and look up at the sign on the building. It says *funeral home*. That's when I realize that I didn't survive the crash after all. I'm dead! It suddenly made sense: the dirt in my mouth, all of it. I'd been buried under the ground."

He laughed nervously. "Talk about lost souls, eh?" Then he exhaled deeply. "That one freaked me out. I woke up with my heart beating like crazy. Messed up, huh?"

Nathaniel leaned back in his chair. "You've had time to reflect on the dream. What do you make of it?"

"I figured you'd ask that. The obvious answer is that's it's about death, I guess, my father's death and how it's affected me."

"You don't sound convinced."

"I don't know. Maybe that's all there is to it. But then I think back to the wreckage and I remember the truck was black. And that gets me thinking about that black Expedition that's been following me."

"Do you still think it's following you?"

Chris gave him a bewildered look. "You ask like you think I'm seeing things that aren't there. I'm telling you, I've seen a black Expedition a handful of times now. That's reality." He could feel himself getting worked up. He drew a deep breath and waited a moment. "Whether it's coincidence that I keep seeing it, I don't know."

"You said you had another dream?"

"Yeah, this one's just as weird. It happens at work. I'm in an interview room with Marilyn—she's the psychiatrist friend at IFP that I've told you about. And there's a nurse and a patient in the room, too. It's a typical meeting. We're talking about how the patient is doing. The creepy thing is that when the meeting's over, everyone else gets up to walk off the unit, but I'm being held back. And I suddenly realize, they think *I'm* the patient. I'm trying to convince everyone that I'm staff, but no one's listening."

He took another deep breath. "Look, Nathaniel, I don't know if this is a waste of time, but you asked me to write my dreams down."

"No, it's certainly not a waste of time. I find it very interesting. What meaning do you attribute to this dream?"

"I'm not sure. But I've been thinking a lot lately about everything that's happened and my reaction to it. I ... I feel like my mind's been working against me."

"How so?"

"Not being able to get Ray out of my head, for

starters. My nightmares. My emotions, I can't seem to control them. There are times when I feel like I have no control over my feelings, and I hate that feeling. It makes me feel powerless, helpless." He stopped and looked over at Nathaniel, embarrassed. "I work in mental health, so believe me, none of this dream is lost on me. What I'm trying to say is that it gets me thinking about someone who's having a breakdown. At what point do they realize they're having one? Most times they don't, you know what I mean? Insight is one of the first things that goes out the window.

"So then I think back to what I'm going through, and there are moments when I realize I have to look after myself. Heck, that's why I'm seeing you, to keep from having a breakdown. But then there are moments when I think everything's pretty much okay, back to normal even, and I wonder what I was so worried about."

He looked away. "I guess the reason that dream disturbs me is that it makes me question my own sanity. Would I know if I was having a breakdown?"

"Well, you're right about one thing: they are very interesting dreams, and I appreciate the fact that you've shared them with me. Do you want me to tell you what I think?"

"Fire away," Chris said, although he was a little afraid to know.

"It seems to me that no matter where you start in your conversation, it ultimately reverts back to Ray.

Have you ever considered the possibility that your biggest enemy may not be Ray, but yourself?"

"What do you mean by that?"

"What I mean is, Ray is sitting in jail, awaiting trial on several serious charges. He can't harm you in any physical way. He does not pose an imminent, viable threat to you now, yet you've built him up in your mind as a formidable enemy. I can understand the threat of psychological harm, but that is something you have a degree of control over. *You* can determine the degree of influence he has over your life, if you choose."

Chris reflected for a moment. "We're back where we started, aren't we? Talking about control."

"Let me change the focus slightly. Are you still having those nightmares involving Ray and his rifle?"

"Yeah, and I've tried that re-imagining exercise you mentioned."

"And?"

"And ..." Chris hesitated. "There was a point on that trail where I had the rifle. I've dreamt recently about that moment where I'm the one with the rifle."

"Aimed at Ray?"

"Yeah. Aimed at Ray."

Nathaniel thought for a moment. "So your nightmares have changed from a situation in which you are feeling powerless and have no control to ones where you're the one in control, you're the one with the rifle. Is that right?"

"Yeah."

"Well, that sounds like progress to me."

Chris just sat there, fumbling with his fingers. "You're not convinced, are you?" Nathaniel asked.

Chris sighed. "It's more than that. In the dream," he started slowly, and then blurted out, "in the dream, I pull the trigger. And that opens up a whole new can of worms for me."

"Because?"

"Because it gets me wondering how different I am from him. He's my half-brother. So do I have the same messed-up DNA running through me as he does? The same psychopathic tendencies?"

"What do you think?"

Chris smiled. "You know, you're doing what Stephanie likes to do. Answering my questions with other questions. I don't know what to think, that's the God-honest truth. I hate Ray with every fibre of my being. I'd like to think that I'm nothing like him, that I'm better than that." He bowed his head and started massaging his temples. "But I'm not so sure. And until I am, I don't want to make any big decisions."

"I'm not sure I'm following you. What decisions are you talking about?"

Chris told Nathaniel about the conversation he'd had with Stephanie about starting a family. "I love Stephanie, I really do. I just think the timing's bad. I don't feel ready to ..." His voice trailed off.

"What do you think would need to change for the timing to be good for you?"

"Right now, I really don't know," Chris said. "But Ray would have to be out of the picture, I can tell you that much."

"Hmm. Ray again. I think we've talked enough about Ray for one day. Let's change the topic. How was your return to work?"

"I managed to get through it, despite hearing that I returned too early." Before Nathaniel had a chance to ask whom he was referring to, Chris said, "Stephanie, Marilyn, my manager. They all think I should have stayed away longer."

"I'm interested right now in what you think."

"They're probably right, on the one hand. But on the other, coming to work gives me something constructive to do with my time rather than sitting at home fiddling with my fingers."

"Do you feel you have it under —"

"There's that word again, *control*," Chris interrupted. "I hope so. What do you think?" He cringed the moment he asked the question because he had a feeling he wasn't going to like the answer.

"From what you've described here today, my opinion is that it would be best for you to take a few weeks off to give your body and mind more rest. I'd suggest a leave of absence. But it's your call."

"Yeah, I'm not really sure about taking time off work."

"Have you shared what you're going through with anyone at your work? Manager, co-workers?"

Chris shook his head, avoiding making eye contact. "My manager and one of my colleagues know I'm seeing a counsellor but that's about it. I haven't gone into details."

"What you're experiencing, Chris, is actually more common than you might think." Nathaniel stopped. He appeared to be waiting for a reaction from Chris and when there was none, he continued. "On top of that, I think it's important to consider your particular work environment. Your work often involves trauma, whether your patients come to you as victims of past trauma or are admitted after being charged with committing an offence with traumatic repercussions. Either way, it exposes you to vicarious trauma."

Nathaniel stopped again, as if inviting Chris to respond. Chris didn't.

"My point is that you're not alone," Nathaniel continued. "Yet many employees are reluctant to talk to their co-workers or managers because they're embarrassed. Or they're concerned that they won't be understood. Or worse yet, that they'll be looked down upon for having a problem. What I'm getting at, Chris, is that I think it might be time to talk to your manager about what you're going through. Would you consider doing that?"

"I'm not ready for that right now. I'd rather keep things between you and me, at least for now."

"Do you mind my asking why?"

Chris adjusted his position in his seat. He realized he was sweating and rubbed his fingers against his clammy palm. His mouth was dry. "Just a second." He stood up to pour himself a glass of water from Nathaniel's cooler. He sat back down and took a few gulps before continuing.

"Reaching out for help is not something that comes naturally to me," he offered. "I know how that sounds, given that I work in a helping profession. It's something I need to work on." He shrugged his shoulders.

Nathaniel gave a supportive smile. "The content of our sessions is confidential. I would only breach that confidence if I had imminent concerns about your safety or that of someone else. But I wouldn't be doing my job if I didn't point out my concern."

"I'll think about it."

Nathaniel looked at his watch. "We've covered a fair amount today. I'd encourage you to reflect on what we talked about and to continue with your dream diary. I'd also like to leave you with a visioning exercise. Would that be okay?"

Chris nodded, and Nathaniel began. "What do you want out of life, Chris?"

"What do I want? What do you mean?"

"If you had the power to make it happen, what would you want to achieve in your life?"

Chris started to think. "I guess I'd want to be happy, to have peace of mind, to not be always looking over my shoulder. Not worrying about the safety of the people I love."

"You said happiness. When you think about the barriers to your happiness, who or what comes to your mind?"

"Ray. That's an obvious one." Then he thought for a moment. "And I guess my mother, in the sense that she's always on my mind. My father, too. And I guess you could say Deanna, my wife. I could have been a better husband, and it bothers me that I couldn't make it work with her, both for the sake of our marriage and for our daughter."

"Then think about these questions. I don't want you to answer them right now. I want you to leave with them on your mind, and I want you to think about them after today. Okay?"

"Okay."

"You mentioned your father. For the sake of your happiness, can you let him go?" He waited a moment before continuing. "And your mother: for the sake of your happiness, can you let her go? Your marriage to Deanna has ended, and from what you've told me, you've both moved on in your relationships and your lives. For the sake of your happiness, can you let her go?

"And finally Ray. Ray is in custody and has no chance of release anytime soon. For the sake of your happiness, can you let him go?"

TWENTY-NINE

Just how do *you let someone go?* Chris reflected in his truck driving home. Someone he loved, in the case of his mother and Deanna. Or in the case of Ray, someone he hated, someone he couldn't afford to let go because it was clear that Ray wasn't about to let *him* go. And he wasn't even sure how he felt about his father anymore.

A few glasses of rum and cola were awfully tempting, but Chris resisted the craving and instead called Stephanie. As he listened to her voice, his troubles slowly faded from his mind, replaced by thoughts of lying next to her. It was going for eight-thirty and they were making plans for a quiet evening when his phone beeped an incoming call. He told Stephanie he'd call her back and answered the other call. It was Deanna.

"Sorry to be phoning on short notice. I'm running behind, at my mother's. Is there any way you could pick Ann Marie up at dance?"

"Sure," he responded instantly.

"I should be home in about an hour or so. Are you okay staying at the house until I get home? You've still got a house key, right?"

This meant a change in plans. He wouldn't be seeing Stephanie tonight after all, but he never passed on an opportunity to see Ann Marie. "That sounds good. Take your time. We'll be fine. And yeah, I've got a key."

"Thanks, Chris. I'm sorry if this fouls anything up for you."

Chris called Stephanie back and apologized for cancelling their plans. He drove to the dance studio on Granville Street, hoping to arrive early enough to catch a few minutes of his daughter's practice. The parking lot was full, but he doubled around and was rewarded for his effort when someone pulled out of a space. He parked his truck and walked quickly toward the building. If he hurried, he'd have a chance to see Ann Marie dancing.

As he neared the studio entrance, he spotted a black Expedition with tinted windows driving down Granville Street in his direction.

Without thinking, he charged toward the vehicle.

"STOP FOLLOWING ME!" he bellowed at the top of his lungs.

He narrowly missed getting clipped by the truck as it passed him. He didn't care, nor did he stop. He continued racing after it and managed to pound his right fist hard on the back window before the vehicle's speed surpassed his. "STAY THE FUCK AWAY!" He looked for a licence number but it was partially obscured with black tape. *Was it to avoid detection?* Chris wondered.

The SUV sped away in the distance, and Chris' exhausted body forced him to stop his pursuit. He was out of breath, and his hand was aching.

His rage ebbed and his mind returned to reality as he slowly limped back to the studio parking lot. An audience of parents and children met him with shocked expressions. One mother clutched her young daughter's hand and hurried to the safety of her minivan, giving Chris a scornful look as she passed him. A father gave him a 'what's your problem?' look.

What broke Chris' heart, though, was the look on Ann Marie's face. In that moment, he wasn't sure whether she was afraid, confused, embarrassed, or some dreadful combination of all three. He felt exactly the same way.

The drive home did little to improve the situation. Chris could tell that his daughter was shaken by the way she clutched her dance bag tight against her body and refrained from being her usual chatty self. He spent the entire time trying to come up with the right words and the right way to tell her why he'd acted the way he did.

But there were no magical words, nothing he could say or do that would justify his behaviour. The best thing he could do, he realized, was discuss his actions honestly with his daughter.

When they finally got home, Chris sat Ann Marie next to him on the living room couch.

"Sometimes, Sweetie, adults make mistakes," he started. "I made a big one today. I thought the person in that truck was following me, and that made me mad. But I shouldn't have acted that way. I'm really sorry." He looked at his daughter to gauge her reaction. She kept staring at the floor.

"I didn't mean to scare you, Sweetie. That's the last thing I'd ever want to do."

"Was ... Was it the bad man from Grandpa's funeral in the truck? I heard Mommy talk about him with Grandma."

"No, Sweetie, it wasn't. The bad man's in jail and can't hurt anybody. But that's not important now," he said, gently kissing her forehead. "You're what's important, and I'm so sorry I missed seeing you dance."

Ann Marie said nothing and retreated to her room.

Chris berated himself, worried that his reckless behaviour would be permanently engraved in Ann Marie's memory. *Great, a new low.*

A few minutes passed and Chris was still struggling to figure out what he should do next to remedy the situation, when Ann Marie emerged from her room and tentatively stood in front of him.

"Do you want to see my dance?"

"I'd love to," he said, his eyes misting.

Chris revelled in watching his daughter perform

her moves. When Deanna arrived home, she joined him, even cozying up next to him while Ann Marie gleefully danced for the two of them. And when it was time for her to go to bed, they took turns reading to Ann Marie from *Ivy and Bean* before turning out her light.

Back in the living room, they talked briefly about the funeral before discussing their daughter's upcoming week of activities, including her dance recital. Chris finally got the nerve to tell Deanna about the incident at the dance studio. He thought her silence spoke volumes.

"I apologized to Ann."

"That's not the point, Chris. You can't have outbursts like that in front of her. It scares her."

"I know. I messed up. Believe me, I know."

"Oh, Chris," Deanna sighed. "I know it's been rough. Your father, and that whole thing with Ray at the funeral. Are you going to be okay?"

"Yeah, I just need to get some rest."

Chris got up to leave. Deanna stopped him with a gentle touch on his shoulder. "It's late and you look tired. You're welcome to stay here tonight."

He felt something stir inside him, a sexual spark he thought had long since been extinguished in their relationship. Was Deanna coming on to him? Or was he misinterpreting this just as badly as he'd misinterpreted the intentions of the SUV driver? He wasn't sure. He wasn't sure about a lot of things anymore.

"Uh, I should be going. Got stuff at my apartment I'll need tomorrow."

He could tell his face was flushed, and he resisted the urge to look Deanna in the eye. He quickly said goodbye and left her house, the house that had once been theirs.

The day's confusing events were taking a toll on him now, and his head was hurting. When he got home, Chris considered having a drink or five. Instead, he popped a couple of ibuprofen and crumpled into bed.

THIRTY

When Chris awoke the next morning, he checked his smartphone to get caught up. He was startled to see a story in the *Tribune* reporting on the review of unescorted patient access to the community. The piece included a statement from IFP director Florence Threader, emphasizing that "public safety is of paramount concern and is never compromised for the sake of patient community reintegration."

He was grateful it was Saturday and not a workday, but he had no intention of staying home to rest his weary body. He had plenty of work of another kind to do.

He texted Stephanie to suggest plans for the evening. No answer.

On his drive to the West Coast Correctional Centre,

he vacillated on whether to abandon his plan or go through with it. He knew that what he was doing was risky, but he had questions that only Ray could answer, and he was going to do his best to get those answers.

At the front desk, he presented his identification to the security guard, fully expecting to be turned away when he told the guard whom he was intending to visit. But to his surprise, Chris was taken through a security screening procedure to ensure he had no weapons or contraband and then was ushered to a secure visiting area where he was told to wait. He used the time to work on controlling the anxiety he was experiencing in anticipation of seeing Ray. Finally, the door opened and two guards escorted Ray into the large room.

"Well, well, what a pleasant surprise," Ray said mockingly. "I thought we weren't supposed to have *direct or indirect contact*. I won't tell, though, if you won't," he added slyly. "I've always considered it more of a guideline than a rule. So, brother dear, what brings you all the way out here? You miss me?"

"Cut the crap," Chris countered, glaring at Ray. "We both know why I'm here. Why did you send someone to spy on me and my daughter?"

Ray leaned back in his chair and stroked the stubble on his chin as though he was giving the question serious consideration. "What, no condolences on my loss?" He gave a look of feigned pain.

"Why've you got people following me?" Chris repeated, the anger clear in his voice.

"Listen to you, brother dear, all paranoid and shit. And look at those bags under your eyes. I sleep like a baby, a baby girl, maybe."

"Stop messing around and answer the question!"

"Why? It's more fun watching you squirm," Ray laughed. He leaned in closer and spoke in a lower voice. "Guess what? I got me a lawyer. A *good* one."

"Bernum doesn't come cheap. Must be costing you a pretty penny."

"Nope. Not paying a cent," Ray boasted. "Turns out I've got friends in low places. Just like the song. He even helped me get a cellphone. *Technically*, it's against the rules but ..." He shrugged. "A guy's gotta survive. It's not as good as my old phone. You remember that one, right?"

"Oh, I remember it, all right. And the cops remember it, too. They're using it right now to collect evidence against you. And there's nothing you or your lawyer will be able to do about it. What the hell were you thinking, anyway? Ever hear of a burner?"

Ray snickered at the defiance in Chris' voice. "I guess we'll have to wait and see. Of course, a lot could happen between now and then. In the meantime, I'm making the most of my time in here. Got a decent TV, three square meals, and no bills to pay. No one bugs me. Not like the mindfuckers at your shithole IFP."

"It's good you like it here, Ray, 'cause it's going to be your home for a long, long time."

"Bullshit, Ryder, you haven't won."

"It's not about winning or losing, Ray. Why can't you get your head around that?"

"You better believe it's about winning. And I'll let you in on something, Ryder. Between detention centres, halfway homes, and jails, I've spent more time on the inside than outside." He gestured to the room they were in. "*This* is like home to me. So your little threat about spending time here doesn't mean squat to me. Just gives me more time to think about the important things in life. Like family, *your* family."

"I swear to God, you go near —"

"You'll do what? Send me to jail?" Ray broke into wild laughter. "Fuck you, Ryder. You had your chance with family, and I had shit. But I'll swear something to *you*. I'll have you looking over your shoulder, worrying about your precious little Ann Marie and your fuck-buddy, Stephanie. I'm gonna be so far in your head, you'll think I'm your shadow! And it ain't gonna stop till it's just you and me."

Chris realized he'd made a mistake in coming and got up to leave.

"Take good care of yourself, brother dear," Ray taunted. "Don't go dying on me. You're the only family I've got left."

The dig triggered something for Chris, something he thought was worth exploring. "But that's not true, is it, Ray?"

"What are you talking about?"

"I'm talking about your foster sister. You have one, don't you? That's what I read in your report."

Ray gave him a look that Chris couldn't quite read. "She wasn't related to me. She was nothing to me but a pain in the ass," he sneered. "Besides, she's not my problem anymore."

"What happened, Ray? You became her shadow, too?" Chris countered, looking for a reaction.

"Something like that." Ray looked Chris straight in the eye.

Chris felt a shiver run down his spine. He spun on his heel and continued walking toward the exit, suddenly sick to his stomach. What had Ray done to his foster sister?

"It's been a nice visit, Ryder," Ray called after him. "Next time, bring your daughter. Oh, and say hi to Stephanie for me. I keep looking for her in here, but I guess she must be avoiding me." Ray's mocking laughter followed Chris out of the room.

As he drove away from the centre, Chris looked in his rear-view mirror, his gaze fixing on the barbed wire on top of the perimeter fence, designed to keep the inmates inside. He thought back to Ray's boast about living a carefree life within the correctional centre. Then he thought about Ray's continued ability to wreak havoc on his life. *Who is the real prisoner?*

THIRTY-ONE

Chris returned home disillusioned. There was still so much he didn't know about Ray, particularly Ray's time in care as a youth and with his foster sister.

He dug through his closet until he found a binder containing documents on Ray he'd received from a colleague from Adult Community Corrections. He searched through the pile of pre-sentence and other court reports until he found the social history on Ray as a youth from the Ministry of Child and Family Development. He'd previously combed through this document trying to locate the social worker who had written the report, eager to know how the information had been obtained. He'd struck out then, but today he was looking for another detail: the name of the foster mother who'd taken Ray in when all his other placements had ended miserably and all other options had been exhausted.

His diligence paid off. And an online search for a Wanda Hill in the Vancouver area yielded four possibilities.

He wrote down the information and started making phone calls. The first number he called was no longer in service, and he left a general message at the home of the second. He was in the middle of leaving a similar message with his third call when someone picked up.

"Hello?" It was a woman's voice. "Who did you say you were looking for?"

"Wanda Hill."

"And what is this in regards to?"

"A person named Raymond. Or Ray." He paused for a moment before continuing. "Ray Owens." He was met with silence but his gut told him he'd reached the right person.

"My name is Chris Ryder. I totally understand why you'd be reluctant to talk about Ray with someone you don't know. I —"

"I know who you are. I've read about you in the news." There was an audible sigh. "I've been wondering when this call would come."

Chris clarified that he was calling personally, not professionally, and Wanda said she understood. She declined Chris' offer of meeting in person. She'd moved three times over the past several years, mostly out of fear that Ray would track her down. However, she agreed to talk with Chris with the understanding that their conversation wouldn't get back to Ray. It unnerved Chris that even after all these years, she still lived in fear of Ray.

"Ask me what you want to know, Mr. Ryder, and I'll see if I can help." Wanda's voice was tired.

He had so many questions that it was hard to decide where to start. "What can you tell me about Ray's biological mother?"

"Nothing, I'm afraid. I wasn't given any information about her at all."

Chris had hoped to learn some, *any* information about Ray's mother. "I read that he came to live with you when he was around ten. Is that right?"

"That's right," Wanda said flatly.

"Can you tell me what led to the decision for him to live with you?"

"Back then, I'd developed a bit of a reputation for working well with the more challenging children that came through my door. The Ministry came to me after Raymond had burned through his other placements. I don't doubt that some of them had been bad. I heard about the abuse he endured. I've always believed that everyone deserves a fresh start and I did my best to give Raymond a good home."

"You mentioned abuse. What do you know about that?"

No response.

"Ms. Hill, I promise I won't tell Ray that we talked. But your information would be very helpful to me."

"Very well," she said with a sigh. "Raymond had a problem with bedwetting. The foster family he was staying with at the time had two children of their own, neither of which, I guess, wet the bed. The parents thought this was acting-out behaviour from Raymond. I was told the father disciplined him using a belt to strap his bottom. The other children were a few years older than Raymond, and they teased him about his bedwetting and told his classmates at school. You can imagine the kind of reaction that led to."

She paused as though she was recalling the unpleasant details. "I heard stories, after the fact, that the parents gave their own children preferential treatment and ignored Raymond, to the point that I guess he learned that the most effective way for him to get attention was by acting out. I suppose you would call that attention-seeking behaviour."

"Do you know what led to his removal from that home?"

"The story, as it was told to me, is that one morning he showed up at school with a bottom so sore he couldn't sit properly in his seat. The teacher brought him to the guidance counsellor, and eventually they pieced together a picture of what was going on at home. I think that placement scarred Raymond for life, psychologically if not physically."

"What happened when he came to you?"

"Jealousy. His behaviour was marginally appropriate as long as all the attention was on him. But the minute he thought he was competing for it, it was over. I took him to counsellor after counsellor, but it made no difference. I lost so much because of him: my pets, my marriage."

"Is it true he killed your bird?"

"Yes."

"And he shot his foster sister in the eye with a pellet gun?"

"Yes." Wanda started to sob. "He hated Teresa with a passion. He was twelve when he shot her. My husband had already left me by then. He was afraid of Raymond. Teresa lost sight in her left eye. That was the final straw. The Ministry removed Raymond from my care."

"What about Teresa? Where is she now?"

Silence. "She was a good girl, but she had her own problems. She would cut herself when she was overwhelmed. And when she was older, she got caught up with drugs. She kept in touch with me over the years through letters. From the last one I received, it sounded like she was turning her life around."

Silence again, followed by heavier sobbing. "I was shocked to hear that she'd overdosed on heroin."

"I'm really sorry to hear that, Ms. Hill. Do you remember when that was?"

"Getting close to five years now. They found her in a hotel room on the Downtown Eastside. She had bruising on her wrists, and they thought there was evidence of a struggle. They didn't think she was alone. That's why I've never believed it was suicide. I've spent so many sleepless nights wondering who was in that room with her. Wondering who would let her die like that."

Chris' chest tightened as he thought of Ray. "Were there any suspects?"

"Not enough evidence. It was passed off as a junkie's overdose."

Chris felt terrible about forcing Wanda to relive these obviously painful memories, but he needed the answers to his questions. "Are you up to answering a few more questions, Ms. Hill? I'm almost finished."

"Go ahead, Mr. Ryder." Her voice was toneless now.

"When was your last contact with Ray?"

She laughed nervously. "The last time I saw him? Or the last time I received a threatening phone call?" She answered before Chris could elaborate. "The last time I saw him was the day the Ministry took him from my house, ages ago. He looked back at me with a big smirk on his face and told me he wouldn't forget me, or Teresa."

"And he called you after that?"

"He called a lot the first several months after he left. That's why I moved and changed my phone number. Months would go by, but he'd always manage to find out my new number and I'd be woken up in the middle of the night by a call from him. Sometimes he'd shout profanities and threats at me, and other times he wouldn't say anything at all although I knew it was him on the line. I gave up changing my phone number after a while. I think he enjoyed the challenge of tracking me down."

"Do you know where he went after you?"

"No. I was too afraid to know. I hoped I'd never hear from him again. And I hadn't for years. But then there was that killing at Woodland Park, and it brought back all those memories for me. Then a social worker called me a few weeks ago, looking for information on Raymond. From what I understand, he has a son."

"He what?" Chris hoped he'd misheard her.

"Sad, isn't it? The social worker said she couldn't disclose much to me because of privacy issues, but she implied that the child's mother wasn't in the picture and she wanted information on Raymond from his time with me. I told her pretty much what I've told you and that was the end of it."

Chris didn't know how to respond to the revelation that Ray had a son. Did Ray even know? He thanked Wanda and apologized again for disturbing her afternoon.

"Just one more thing," she said before they ended the call. "I tried my best to help him. For years, I blamed myself. I constantly wondered if I could have done more. I even got counselling for myself. The therapist told me she suspected Raymond had narcissistic personality disorder. She said Raymond was extremely sensitive about rejection. All I know now is, some people can't be helped, and sadly, he's one of them. But I suspect you know that already, Mr. Ryder. I hope you also know to be careful around him."

THIRTY-TWO

Chris reflected on the information he'd gathered from Wanda Hill. Did Ray kill his foster sister? Chris knew only too well that the man was capable of murder, but the possibility that he'd killed Teresa was chilling. He considered what Wanda had said about Ray's jealousy toward Teresa and recalled Ray's jealous rage at Chris' being raised by his biological family while Ray had been placed in foster care.

But what had happened to Ray's mother? How did she meet Maurice, and where was she now? He desperately wanted the answers to these questions, too.

But the biggest surprise of the afternoon was learning that Ray had a son. Who was the mother, and where was she now? Chris started thinking about the son. He wondered how old he was and where *he* was now.

His thoughts were interrupted by a call from Brandon. "Hey, are you gonna be around for a while? Thought I'd check in on how you're doing."

Chris was looking forward to seeing Stephanie but would always make time for his friend. "I can be. What's up?"

"I'll tell you when I get there. Should be maybe thirty minutes."

It was closer to forty-five minutes before Brandon knocked at the door. "Wow, I love what you haven't done with the place," he joked as he scanned the bare apartment. "You have any beer?"

"Good question. Don't know." Chris walked over to the fridge, opened it and saw that he had two Granville Island Pilsners left. He handed one to Brandon and opened the other for himself. "Cheers."

Brandon laughed. "I'm guessing Stephanie doesn't spend much time here."

"Did you come all the way over here to offer interior decorating advice?"

"Nah. I got an update on the Goodwin case, though. Interested?"

"Damn right. What is it?"

Brandon took a gulp of his beer before continuing. "Samples of the blood found at the crime scene were sent to the lab. The results came back today, and I talked to the officer in charge of the file. Two different blood types, but Goodwin's isn't one of them."

Chris gave him a confused look. "But Marvin was found at the scene covered in blood."

"He had blood on his clothes, but it wasn't his, and his blood wasn't found on the victim or the weapon, the tire iron. In fact, there's no trace of his blood anywhere at the scene. Just the victim's and a third person's, and this person has no record in our system."

"So Marvin wasn't there alone?"

"Sure looks that way."

Chris ran the possibilities through his head. "That would explain how he ended up in the middle of nowhere." An idea popped in his head. "Do you think it could be his brother's? Maybe that's why no one can find the brother now. He's hiding."

"Don't know at this point."

"What does this mean for the charge against Marvin?"

"For starters, his lawyer has a strong argument to have the murder charge dropped. We still don't know the role he played in the offence, but now the focus shifts to finding the person matching the blood type."

Chris had his own news and told Brandon about the two addresses he'd received from Marvin. "I think the first one is the house where he lived with his brother. I drove by, and it looks abandoned. I don't know about the second one, though. Do you want them?"

"Sure," Brandon said, seeming to be taken aback. "I'll pass it along to the officer in charge of Goodwin's file."

Chris rifled through his messenger bag until he found the paper with the two addresses. "I know I should have given this to you earlier. To be honest, I was embarrassed." He told Brandon about his trips to the houses.

"So you're a cop, now?" Brandon laughed. "But seriously, you could've gotten yourself in a world of trouble."

"I know," Chris said sheepishly. "Marvin's brother's name is Michael. I Googled him but nothing came up. And when I plugged in the address for the second house, the name Calvin Johnson came up. I Googled that name and a bunch of different Calvins came up, but nothing else stood out."

"Quite the detective work. Thanks." Brandon put the paper in his pocket. "By the way, I see your place has been in the news again. What's the deal with your guys out on day passes, anyway? Aren't you afraid they're gonna take off and land themselves in more trouble?"

Chris felt his blood pressure starting to rise. He wasn't much in the mood for debating the day-leave moratorium with Brandon. He'd learned this was one area where they held opposing views.

"It's complicated."

But Brandon wasn't about to let it go. "What's so

complicated about locking the doors to your hospital? The last thing we need is a bunch of Ray Owenses running loose!"

"Come on, Brandon. First of all, if you remember, Ray isn't at IFP."

"But he tried, didn't he? A lot of them do, trying to fake mental illness, trying to be found not criminally responsible to avoid jail, so they can go to your cushy little hospital and get out on passes. Isn't this what the whole issue is about?"

"No, it's not. The reality is the NCR finding makes up a small fraction of criminal cases. You know why? Because the psychiatric assessment and court processes weed out fakers like Ray. And if you looked at the research, you'd know that many people found NCR actually end up being detained longer in hospital for treatment than if they'd gone to jail. But no one ever talks about that. Or the fact that the re-offending rate for people found NCR is much, much lower than for the general prison population. That's because the forensic psychiatric system works!"

"You don't need to get defensive with me, Chris. I'm just trying to understand the logic behind letting someone go out on his own after you yourself have said he's mentally ill, hearing voices and the like."

"We don't just open the door and cross our fingers hoping that nothing bad happens, Brandon. Patients go through many steps, starting with assessment outings with staff to make sure they're ready. *Then* they have several staff-supervised outings, *before* gradually getting unsupervised access to the community. And there are safeguards and contingency plans in place at every step of the way. And if it's felt that the risk from a patient can't be managed, he doesn't go out in the first place."

"But you wouldn't have *any* risk if you didn't let him out at all, is all I'm saying. I end up having to deal with them on the street."

"Yeah, I know how that ends. The Tanner case."

Neil Tanner, a distraught young man with a history of mental illness, had been shot to death by two police officers a year earlier after he'd lunged at them with a baseball bat. The incident had been captured on a smartphone and posted to YouTube, where it went viral and created an uproar in Vancouver and beyond, with accusations of excessive force and police brutality. An inquiry into the incident reinforced the need for mandatory training for all police officers in crisis intervention and de-escalation when interacting with people in mental health distress.

"Hey, that's bullshit, Chris. I've had the training. But there's a world of difference between a classroom and the street when you're in a life-and-death situation without proper backup and without options like tasers at hand."

"You're right. I was out of line." Chris took a deep breath. As frustrated as he was, he knew a lot of people were asking the same questions as Brandon. He also knew Brandon was a good cop—and his friend. "I guess it all comes down to whether we're about incarceration or rehabilitation. Do we lock people up because they have a mental illness, or do we help them recover and return successfully to their communities? The reality is that high-risk offenders don't account for the majority of the patients I work with, and besides, they're not the ones getting day leaves. Unfortunately, though, it's these extreme few who've gotten all the attention. Like you said, it's the Rays of the world that people are thinking about, but every patient ends up getting tarred with the same brush. The result breeds fear about anyone with a mental illness."

"Yeah, well, good luck with changing people's attitudes."

Chris sensed Brandon was still bristling from his earlier remark about the Tanner case. "Hey, I'm sorry. I shouldn't have said what I said."

Brandon's nod suggested all was forgiven, and they finished their beer in companionable silence as Chris reflected on Marvin's case. "Do you ever think about the randomness of life?" he asked suddenly.

Brandon gave him a puzzled look. "In what way?"

"I mean, take Mr. Bianchi. He loses his life and Marvin ends up at IFP charged with his murder, all because of the breakdown of an ice cream truck. Can you believe that? If the truck hadn't broken down, Mr. Bianchi wouldn't have been stuck on the side of the road and maybe none of this would have happened."

Chris shook his head. "And Ray's cellphone. If I hadn't found it in that park, I would never have run into him and I wouldn't be in the situation I'm in today."

"And we wouldn't have met," Brandon pointed out, continuing the line of reasoning. He sighed deeply. "Yeah, I've thought a lot about fate, too. You can drive yourself crazy thinking about the what-ifs in life."

Unable to shake Ray from his thoughts, Chris found himself wishing he could what-if his nemesis out of existence, but he settled for telling Brandon about his call to Ray's former foster mother, sharing the news about Ray's foster sister's death and the fact that Ray had a son. "He leaves a path of destruction wherever he goes," Chris said in disgust. "It makes me wonder what life would be like if I'd killed him when I had the chance. It would have been self-defence and he'd be nobody's problem anymore."

"You want to know how I got this?" Brandon pointed to a faint scar that started above his eye and continued down toward his cheekbone.

Chris nodded. He'd wondered before about the scar but hadn't wanted to pry.

"One night, my partner and I got a call about an armed robbery. When we arrived, one of the perps came at me with a seven-inch knife. He took a pretty decent swing at me, connected above my eye right here." Brandon pointed to the faded scar. "I kicked him on his ass and drew my revolver, told him to stay put.

But he got up, looked like he was high on something, started to charge me. I shot him ... dead." He stopped, took a slow breath before continuing. "So, what you said earlier about the Neil Tanner case kinda hit me hard."

"I didn't mean to stir up bad memories."

"Don't worry about it," Brandon responded soberly. "There was an investigation, and I was cleared. Self-defence. If I hadn't shot him, there's a good chance I wouldn't be here today. I was trained to shoot to kill in situations like that." A look of pain crossed his face. "But I've lost track of how many nights I've spent wondering whether I could have handled things differently, whether I could have fired a less lethal shot at him. Truth is, I'll never know. I was pissed at him, and well, I was scared that he was going kill me." He sighed. "All I know is that I'm reminded every time I look in the mirror. Believe me, you don't want that kind of thing on your conscience. It eats away at you."

"I hear what you're saying, but there are also times when I'm terrified that Ray will find a way around the legal system somehow, especially with Bernum taking his case. Would you have confidence that the legal system would deal with someone like him? Or would you take care of it yourself?"

Brandon shrugged. "All I know is, once you cross the line, there's no going back. We end up being no better than the criminals we're after." He looked at his empty bottle and gave a heavy sigh. "I should go. Let you get back to sprucing up your place."

THIRTY-THREE

Long after Brandon had gone, Chris continued thinking about their conversation. He decided he needed a run to burn off his nervous energy. He changed into his running gear and left his apartment for the streets of his neighbourhood.

Adrenalin rushed through his body and it didn't take long to find his rhythm. But it wasn't only the physical high from running that he was looking for. Running also helped him slow down his thoughts and focus his mind.

Today's run had him thinking about the black SUV. *Was it the same vehicle he saw each time? Was it following him?* Knowing the licence plate would go a long way toward answering his questions, but he had only had a partial plate number. He suddenly figured out a way he might be able to track down the vehicle and fist-pumped the air in celebration of his breakthrough.

By the time he got home, Chris was physically tired but mentally energized. He was excited at the prospect of identifying the driver of the SUV, but tonight, his anticipation was reserved for his evening with Stephanie. He quickly showered, dressed, and drove to her condo.

After a brief deliberation, Stephanie and Chris ordered in from a local Chinese restaurant. While they ate, they caught each other up on their days. Stephanie talked enthusiastically about the positive feedback her manager had given about the group she was running. As Chris listened to her spirited voice and saw the sparkle in her eyes, he found himself overcome with love for her. *This* moment, *this* feeling was one he wished he could hold onto and never let slip from his memory.

Stephanie poked him in the arm. "You're not listening to a word I'm saying, are you?"

"I was, I am. *Really*," he said sheepishly, his cheeks flushed. "Okay. You want to know what I was thinking?"

She nodded.

"I was thinking how lucky I am to have you. It doesn't matter what we're doing. We could be folding laundry for all I care. I'd be the happiest guy in the world because we'd be together."

"Are you telling me you want to fold laundry?" she teased, but her eyes were misting over.

He ignored her wisecrack. "You have to hear this." He pulled out his smartphone and scrolled down his artists' icons until he landed on Pearl Jam. "This song is from a sound check in Italy during their tour in '06." He walked over to her sound dock, pressed a few buttons and "Faithful" started playing.

He motioned for Stephanie to join him on the couch and wrapped his arm around her. They listened in silence to Eddie Vedder's powerful delivery of the song until it was over.

"Right now, this is one of my favourites," Chris said. "It doesn't matter what kind of day I'm having. I play this and I automatically feel better." He locked eyes with Stephanie. "I love the fact that I can share this with you. It's how I feel about *us*."

"Are you saying you're always going to be faithful?" she joshed.

"What I'm saying is that my world is empty without you and I love being with you."

Stephanie's eyes glistened. "You're staying tonight." She kissed him passionately. "And I'm not taking no for an answer."

THIRTY-FOUR

What am I going to do?

The question had been clanging relentlessly inside Chris' head since four in the morning, making it impossible for him to fall back to sleep. He was lying in a warm bed next to the woman he loved. So why couldn't he enjoy this moment and shake the feeling of impending doom?

Chris watched Stephanie's peaceful, rhythmic breathing. How could he protect her? He couldn't shake the feeling of danger that permeated his life. Were the people he loved safe? His heart was hammering in his chest, heralding another anxiety attack. He tried his breathing exercises, but to no effect. He attempted to distract himself by visualizing a comforting, safe place. *But what do you do when your safe place itself is under attack? Is there refuge anywhere?* He finally sprang out of bed, defeated and enraged.

"What's wrong?" Stephanie asked sleepily.

"Gotta get some air. Sorry to wake you." He retreated to her living room, opened the sliding door to her balcony, and stepped out. The cold, damp night air hit him hard.

"Another bad night?" Stephanie asked, joining him on the terrace, a white cotton robe draped around her body.

Her presence startled him. "Yeah," he finally said. "Unfortunately."

He walked back to the living room, and Stephanie followed. "Do you want to talk about it?"

"Not much to talk about. I shouldn't have stayed over. Now I've screwed up your sleep, too."

"I don't care about that. I'm more worried about you, Chris. Talk to me. Let's work through it together."

"What is there to say, Stephanie? I'm trying, I'm going to counselling. But I'm still having panic attacks and I still have nightmares. It's frustrating."

"I know that, Chris, and you're doing the right thing with seeing Nathaniel. But healing takes time."

"It sure does." He started to get dressed.

"Where are you going?"

"Home. I'm really sorry."

He left her condo. With every step away from Stephanie, he wondered if he was making the biggest mistake of his life.

Chris stopped to load up on caffeine at a Starbucks on the drive back from Stephanie's condo. He had a whole day to kill before the Canucks game. What should have been a source of joy and excitement now felt more like a dreadful obligation. In his current mood, he didn't feel like doing anything with anybody. Even running was too gargantuan a task. Instead, he decided to spend the next few hours trying to distract himself from his worries by listening to music. It didn't take long for him to doze off.

It also didn't take long before he was jolted awake by disturbing images of rotting corpses. He gave up on sleep and rolled out of bed. Searching through his cluttered closet until he found his dated Canucks jersey—emblazoned with a 10 for Pavel Bure—he threw it on and got ready for the game. He figured that finding a parking spot near the arena would be next to impossible on game night and decided to take the SkyTrain near his apartment to downtown Vancouver. The minute he arrived at the Metrotown platform, he realized he'd made an enormous mistake. Hordes of passengers were clumped together jostling for the few remaining spaces on the train that had just arrived. He didn't board that train, deciding instead to take his chances on the next one being less crowded. All the while, he was acutely aware of his rapidly increasing heartbeat. The crowds, the noise, and the overwhelming tension had Chris feeling as if he was going to pass out.

Staggering over to a less-crowded part of the platform, he managed to brace himself against the wall before lowering his body to the ground. He closed his eyes and massaged his aching head, waiting for the moment to pass.

"Hey, what are you doing there?" A Transit Police officer stood over Chris, eyeing him suspiciously.

"Uh ... don't ... feel good," was all Chris could manage in his present state.

"Well, go somewhere else. No loitering here."

Chris was oblivious to what the officer was saying. His head felt as if it were going to spin off his body.

"Get up! Move on!"

Chris looked up and saw that a crowd was forming around them now as passengers became alerted to the scene developing before them. He heard taunts and catcalls, mostly toward the officer. The man used his radio to call for backup and was quickly joined by another officer who moved in to disperse the mass of people.

The first officer briefed his partner on his interaction with Chris, summing up his encounter with "Probably a mental patient off his meds or a druggie. Either way he's not cooperating."

The second officer, appearing more sympathetic, leaned slightly down toward Chris, who remained hunched on the ground. "What seems to be the problem, sir?"

Chris was finally starting to come around. He

summoned enough energy to say, "No problem," then took a deep breath and slowly rose to his feet. He looked at the first officer. "For your information, I'm not a 'mental patient' or a 'druggie.' But what if I was? That's how you treat people?" He walked away, incensed and embarrassed in equal measure.

A train approached the station, and he started walking toward it, but his anxiety worsened with every step. The thought of stepping onto a crowded train and into an even more crowded and emotionally charged hockey arena sent shivers up and down his spine. He texted Horace to say that he'd had a family emergency and apologized for having to miss the game.

He retreated back to his apartment, but not before making a pit stop at a nearby liquor store in a desperate attempt to numb himself.

He knew from his first sip of rum and cola that it would not be his last, as he drank with reckless abandon.

THIRTY-FIVE

Chris was slow in coming to his senses the next morning. The ache in his head was surpassed only by his sense of shame. He tried to shake it off with a hot shower and strong coffee before heading to work.

He approached Horace at the reception desk with a guilty look on his face. "Sorry I bailed on you last night. How much do I owe you?"

"Don't worry about it. I had no problem selling the ticket. It's the freakin' playoffs, man! You missed a good one, though. They're right back in it."

"Yeah, I caught the highlights."

"It's not the same as being there, Chris, but maybe next time. Oh, and I managed to get this for ya." He reached into his desk and handed an official Canucks program to Chris.

"Thanks, I appreciate it." Then, looking at the program, "I know someone who'll appreciate this even more."

After checking his voicemail messages, he grabbed a few art supplies from a stationery cabinet and hurried to Alpha Unit for a meeting about Marvin. Dr. Stevenson updated them on her phone conversation with the Crown Attorney assigned to Marvin's case. First, that forensics had confirmed that the blood found at the scene of Mr. Bianchi's murder did not belong to Marvin, and second, that the Crown was re-examining the charges filed against Marvin in light of this new development. Chris did his best to act surprised, not wanting to tell them Brandon had already shared the news with him. He did, however, express his suspicion that the mystery person's blood might belong to Marvin's brother.

"Do you think Marvin could be covering for his brother?" Alex asked.

"The lawyer said the police are wondering the same thing. I told him that the way Marvin presents to us appears to be genuine and I certainly haven't seen anything that suggests he's overplaying his illness. Have either of you noticed anything?"

Both Alex and Chris shook their heads.

"What role Marvin's brother plays in this case is an interesting question, but one that is ultimately up to the police, and them alone, to determine." She looked pointedly at Chris, giving him the distinct impression

242   D.B. CAREW

she was sending him a message. "Now, are we ready to see Marvin?"

Alex left the room to get the young man.

When they were alone, Dr. Stevenson gave Chris a stern look. "Florence came to my office this morning. Did you *really* go to Marvin's house? You look terrible, by the way."

"Uh ... yeah." His face flushed with embarrassment. "How did Florence know?"

Dr. Stevenson shook her head in disbelief. "She received a call from the RCMP. They said you provided one of their officers with a possible address for Marvin, along with a second address for person or persons unknown, *and* that you had done this after visiting the homes yourself. They asked Florence if it's standard procedure for staff to visit the homes of patients under criminal investigation. So naturally, Florence asked me the same question."

"What did you tell her?" Chris could feel the familiar Florence-related anxiety stirring inside him. He didn't need any more trouble from the director, not now.

Dr. Stevenson paused for a long moment. Chris suspected she wanted to let him sweat a little. Finally she said, "I told her that sometimes the process of collecting collateral information on our patients involves home visits."

Chris let out a sigh of relief. "Thanks, Marilyn."

Now it was Dr. Stevenson's face that turned red.

"Do you realize how reckless and dangerous your actions were? Did you tell anyone you were going there?"

Chris shook his head.

"I didn't think so. There's a rationale behind our policies on home visits and working alone in the community. If anything had happened to you, nobody would have known where you were. This is so unlike you, Chris."

"I know. It was an impulsive move on my part."

"Chris, this is a murder investigation! If Marvin's brother *is* involved and you showed up at his front door, you could have gotten yourself killed! What you did is more than impulsive. It illustrates profound poor judgement."

"I know. I —" he started to say, only to be interrupted by the arrival of Marvin and Alex.

Dr. Stevenson changed her tone and proceeded to ask Marvin a series of simple, yes-or-no questions about his past few days on the unit. Was he sleeping okay? Was he eating okay? Was he having any problems with any of the other patients? Marvin responded to each question with a slight shake of his head, while avoiding direct eye contact with the psychiatrist. He appeared anxious to end the interview and kept looking toward the door, ready to leave, until he spotted the object in Chris' hand.

Chris took the cue. "Marvin, a friend got me this program from the Canucks game." He felt his face burn hot as he thought back to the previous evening's fiasco and how he'd dealt with it. "I know you like to review the stats on the players. This program has some pretty cool ones. Would you like it?" He offered it to Marvin.

"Like it." The young man's eyes lit up, and he pulled the booklet from Chris' hand.

Chris offered to join Alex in accompanying Marvin back to his room, partly because he wanted to avoid further interrogation from Dr. Stevenson and partly because he had a question he wanted to ask Marvin when she wasn't there. Once they were in the main common room of the unit, Chris motioned to Alex that he needed a minute alone with Marvin. Alex moved out of earshot, and Chris took Marvin over to a table.

"Marvin, do you remember the car you were in when you stopped at the ice cream truck?"

"Truck," he repeated in a monotone voice.

"Yes, truck. You know, Marvin, I've heard you're really good at drawing. Can you draw a picture of the car you were in?"

Chris reached into his bag and produced a package of crayons, which he handed to Marvin along with a sheet of paper. The young man pulled out a crayon and immediately started drawing. When he was done, he laid the crayon on the table.

"That's great, Marvin. Can you add the colour of the vehicle?" Marvin rummaged through the box and pulled out another crayon and proceeded to colour.

Chris' heart rate jumped so rapidly he could feel his head getting woozy when he saw the picture Marvin had drawn: a black SUV.

"Okay, one more question, Marvin. Can you draw the licence plate number for that vehicle?" Without hesitation, Marvin wrote a series of letters and numbers depicting a British Columbia licence plate.

Chris thanked him and motioned to Alex that it was okay to take Marvin back to his room. Meanwhile, he looked at the drawing as though it contained the winning numbers for a million-dollar lottery ticket. The sketch reinforced what he'd suspected all along. He actually *had* been followed. Marvin's drawing, complete with a licence plate number, brought Chris a step closer to finding out who was behind that SUV and why he was being followed. Maybe it would also clear Marvin as a suspect in Mr. Bianchi's murder and reveal the identity of the real killer.

Chris could hardly contain his excitement as he made his way to see his patient Paul Butler.

Nursing staff on Beta Unit had left Chris a message that Paul wanted to see him. As he passed the common room, he spotted two patients and a healthcare worker huddled around the TV watching highlights from last night's Canucks game, engaged in a spirited discussion about the game. He checked in with Marissa in the nursing station.

"Okay if I talk with Paul out here?" he asked, pointing to the empty dining area.

Marissa nodded. "Sure, we don't have anything going on right now, but the peer support worker will be running a group there in about an hour. I'll get Paul." She returned a couple minutes later with Paul. He walked to where Chris was sitting and took a seat opposite him. Marissa headed back to the nursing station.

"I heard you wanted to talk with me," Chris said.

"Is there any news on the day leaves?"

"I haven't heard anything new." Chris saw the dejected look on Paul's face. "Is everything okay?"

"Not really. Things were going really good for me at the clubhouse. First they offered me more hours, but I couldn't take them because I had no day passes. Now they're saying they put in a good word for me on a job, a *real, cool* job that I could have transferred to back home, but I can't do anything about it because I can't get day passes for an interview."

"I'm really sorry, Paul. I can look into whether our staff can take you for the interview, at least."

"I'm not even the guy who went UA, yet I'm getting punished for it. We all are. It's not fair."

"I know. It's frustrating." Chris wanted to say more but figured he'd already made enough of a target of himself with administration.

"Do you know when I'll be transferred to Omega Unit?"

Chris shook his head. He knew the wait-list for the discharge program was long. The Omega program consisted of five self-contained cottages located on the hospital grounds. Each cottage housed five patients, responsible for their own medication management, cooking, and house upkeep, providing an opportunity to demonstrate their independent living skills. "You're pretty high on the list though."

"Yeah," Paul said in a subdued tone. "I feel ready to leave. I just want to be able to show it, so that I can go home. I've got a basement suite at my mom's house. And a potential job lined up."

"I know, and it shouldn't take too long. I've spoken with your mother and I've been in contact with the Nanaimo Out-Patient Clinic. They're the ones you'll be working with when you return to Courtenay. You did really well with the programs you've taken and with the staff-escorted outings in the community. The next step, when day leaves are reinstated, is unescorted access to the community. Once you've gone out a few times we'll have a meeting with your mother and the clinic to plan for a visit leave to your home."

"Do you think it could happen in a few months?"

"If things continue the way they have been, that sounds very doable."

There was a long moment of silence. "I want to leave here so badly. I want to see my mom and get on with my life. I don't hear voices anymore. I feel good, I really do. But," he paused briefly, "there's a part of me that's afraid of getting sick again." He looked at Chris, crestfallen. "You wouldn't understand."

"Actually, I do." Chris was surprised with his own response, but continued. "After Ray's attack, I had flashbacks, panic attacks, trouble sleeping. I went to see someone to talk about what I was going through, hoping it would get better. I thought it *was* getting better. I'd have a few good days and think everything was fine. But then I'd have a bad day, and I knew it wasn't over. It's taken me a long time to realize that I'm still working my way through this, and it's going to take even more time before I'm in control again. Sound familiar?"

Paul slowly nodded. "I just want things to go back to the way they used to be, before all this happened. You know?"

"I know. It's tempting to forget the past. In some ways, that's good, but in other ways, it's important to remember. That way, you can learn from it and prevent it from happening again."

Paul remained silent for a moment. "A lot of the guys in here don't have much contact with family. Guess I'm lucky."

"You are, and the plan to live with your mother sounds good. Paul, you've done amazing work and made some really positive gains. The day leaves will be back soon and you'll be able to get out on some passes, and then on visit leave home. You'll get there."

"Yeah, I know." He started to smile. "Thanks."

After Paul left to return to his room, Chris sat and thought. He hadn't realized until his conversation with Paul how much he'd been in denial about his own struggles. His hangover made it impossible to ignore any longer. What he still had to work out was what he was going to do about it. *Was seeing Nathaniel enough?*

Chris returned to his office and called Brandon.

"Remember that SUV I thought was following me?" he asked excitedly.

"Yeah. What about it?"

"I'm pretty sure I've got its licence plate. Will you take it?"

"Fire away."

Chris gave him the information.

"Just out of curiosity, Chris, how did you get this?"

"Marvin," Chris responded with pride. "He has an amazing eye for detail. It dawned on me that if *anyone* was going to remember a licence plate, it would be Marvin."

"I thought he didn't talk much."

"He doesn't, but he's really good about remembering facts, including house numbers and streets. I knew he had to have gotten to the ice cream truck somehow, so I asked him to draw a picture of the car that drove him there, and he drew a black SUV. He's the reason this case is going to crack open!"

"And he gave you the plate number, too?"

"Yep."

"And you think it's the same SUV that's been following you?"

"Come on, Brandon. What are the chances it's not? That would be one hell of a coincidence."

"All right. Now here's a question for you. Have you thought your theory through to its logical conclusion?"

"What do you mean?"

"If you were, in fact, being followed and this turns out to be linked to the crime, you've been followed by a murderer. Or the murderer's accomplice."

"Uh ... I know." Chris' voice started to shake. On an intellectual level, he'd considered this, but hearing the theory posited out loud by someone else now was nonetheless unsettling. "I'm thinking it's Marvin's brother. It has to be. That's why I want you to have the licence plate so you can run it through."

"I'll give this information to the officer involved with the file. But Jesus, Chris, you'd better be careful. You could get caught in the middle of a dangerous situation."

"Yeah, I know. On the other hand, the driver of the SUV is the one who should be careful because he's close to getting caught."

"You better hope you're right."

THIRTY-SIX

The conversation with Brandon and the aftershocks from the last few days, not to mention his raging hangover, left Chris fighting to concentrate on his work. Even an application for legal aid for a newly admitted patient, normally a routine exercise, was beyond his mastery. He stayed in his office with his door closed. His mind raced, jumping from one question to another. *Was Marvin's brother connected to the murder of Mr. Bianchi? Why would he abandon Marvin?*

His head started to throb. Thoughts about his mother and father crept in, exacerbating his headache. He'd struggled for years to cope in the absence of his mother, but now he had the added burden of knowing her murder had not been a random act.

Finally, his workday came to an end. He had but one plan for his evening: visiting his mother's gravesite. It had been years since he'd paid his respects, and he hoped this would bring him some closure.

It was dusk when he reached Grandview Cemetery, situated on a large expanse of land with a spectacular view of the North Shore Mountains and the Pacific Ocean. Light drizzle was falling. A glance around the perimeter confirmed he was alone in the graveyard.

He bowed his head to pray, but no words came to him. The tears did, though, and he watched as they fell onto the bronze plaque bearing his mother's name.

His stress-filled days and sleepless nights had finally caught up with him. He knelt down beside the grave markers and wept.

The graves surrounding him reminded Chris that he was the only living soul in the cemetery now, and he couldn't help but wonder when he would be joining the legions of the dead here. He remembered Ray's threats against him and his family. He was tired of fighting, tired of looking over his shoulder in fear of the unknown.

He considered Nathaniel's question: *For the sake of your happiness, can you let Ray go?* His dark thoughts turned to the stages of grief—denial, anger, bargaining, depression, acceptance—and how they applied to him and Ray. He had first tried denying the threat that Ray posed to him. He'd also had his share of anger against Ray. He knew there was no hope of negotiating with the likes of Ray, and Chris wondered now if he was in the throes of depression.

And he had slowly and soberly arrived at the final stage: acceptance. He knew he couldn't go on like this anymore. He'd have to find a way to let Ray go.

The drizzle turned to rain, pulling Chris back to his cold reality. He texted Stephanie that he loved her, and slowly walked through the shadowy graveyard to return to his truck.

The rain was falling hard now, pelting the dark, empty streets and obscuring Chris' vision as he made his way home. More than anything, he longed for sleep. He wanted to turn his brain off, to escape his life for a while, to finally sleep in peace.

The crash came without warning: a thunderous smash of metal on metal. His truck was hit hard from behind, and the collision propelled it forward, sending it spinning out of control. Chris instinctively slammed his foot on the brake and watched helplessly as he careened toward a large embankment. He braced for impact as the truck smashed into the concrete traffic barrier before finally coming to a violent stop.

He was in shock. His head was spinning, his neck was stiff, and it seemed like needles were piercing his shoulders. He felt himself slipping into unconsciousness.

Through his unclear state, he saw two men approaching. He felt them lift him from the mangled wreck, but he couldn't make out what they were saying and whether they were talking to him or to each other.

His last thought before he passed out: friend or foe?

THIRTY-SEVEN

Chris slowly regained consciousness and tried to take stock of his surroundings. He didn't know how long he'd been out. His hands were tied in front of him and he was sitting in the back seat of a running vehicle, its other two occupants talking intently to each other in the front.

He gently moved his bound hands up to relieve his aching forehead and his fingers came back wet with blood. Who were these people? And where were they taking him? He listened to their conversation.

"... should have left him alone ... What are we gonna do now?"

"What I should've done in the first place!"

Chris' chest felt like it was going to cave in as his mind finally processed where he was: the black SUV.

So he'd been right all along about being followed! The realization came as cold comfort to him now.

The driver glanced at his rear-view mirror and saw that Chris was conscious and staring back at him. "You know how much trouble you've caused me?" He glared at Chris' reflection. "It ends tonight!"

"Come on, Calvin. Don't do something stupid." The passenger sounded worried.

"I'll do what I fucking want."

Calvin turned around to look at Chris, eyes filled with rage. "This is your fault. Sniffing around my place. You think I didn't see that? Now you got the pigs sniffing around there, too. They had nothing on me. Nothing, until you!" He slammed his hand against the steering wheel.

Chris looked at the passenger door with desperate thoughts of escape. But the door had an automatic child lock, operated by the driver.

He looked out the window and recognized where they were headed. The entrance to Woodland Park was less than a minute away. He knew they weren't going there for a late-night stroll.

He was in serious trouble. Before the police linked the SUV to the murder of Bianchi, Chris knew that he too would be dead. At Woodland Park, no less. The irony wasn't lost on him, and he smiled bitterly. He wondered how he was going to survive this, and tried to repress his growing panic by doing his breathing exercises.

As the vehicle entered the dark, empty parking lot, Chris listened to the crunching sound of tires running over pebbles on the gravel road. When the SUV came to a stop, Chris was in the middle of a full-blown panic attack. His shortness of breath left him fighting for air, and his chest hurt like hell. In a moment of morbid curiosity, he wondered if a heart attack would do him in before a bullet would.

The realization hit him that he'd never see Ann Marie again. Or Stephanie.

"Get out," Calvin ordered, disengaging the lock on the back door. He turned in his seat and pointed a .44 Magnum revolver at Chris' head while his passenger got out, came around to Chris' side of the vehicle, and opened the door.

Chris stepped out into the rain.

"You remember this place, doncha?" Calvin mocked as he joined the other two men next to the car.

Chris had never seen either man before, but it was obvious they knew about him.

Calvin caught Chris surveying the SUV's demolished bumper. "Hey, asshole, don't worry about my ride. You got bigger problems to worry about."

"Come on, Calvin, killing him is only gonna make things worse," the second man cautioned. Chris realized now that his voice sounded familiar. Where had he heard it, though?

A memory flickered in Chris' mind. He knew he had one last chance for survival. He had to make the most of it. He looked at Calvin. "Michael's got a point. Killing me won't solve your problem."

"Huh? How do you know his name?" Calvin demanded. Michael looked equally surprised.

"We go back," Chris bluffed. "Him and his brother, Marvin."

"What the fuck is going on?" Calvin shouted, pointing the gun at Chris' head while stealing a suspicious side glance at Michael.

"Take it easy," Michael responded. "He's bullshitting you. We don't know each other. I called him when Marv got admitted to that psych hospital."

"Are you crazy? Why'd you do that?" Calvin took a step away from Michael, as though he were weighing whether he could trust him.

"I didn't say anything about what happened," said Michael. "I just wanted to make sure they took care of Marv. That's all."

"We are taking good care of your brother. More than you did," Chris fired back at him. "You left him there alone to take the fall."

"That wasn't my fault," Michael said defensively. "I had no idea about any of this until after it went down. He wasn't even supposed to be there!"

Michael must have seen the confused look on Chris' face. "Calvin came to my house. I wasn't there, but for some fucked-up reason, he decided to take Marvin for a joyride." He glared at Calvin.

"We've been over that a million times already,"

Calvin countered. "You had him cooped up in that house all the time. I thought I was doing the kid a favour, getting him out, going to my place, having fun for a change."

"Marv hardly ever leaves the house, and he *never* goes without me!"

"Hey, we were having a good time. He was the one who wanted the damn ice cream. Wouldn't shut up about it. 'Ice cream, ice cream,'" Calvin distorted his voice mockingly. "Everything would've been fine if that vendor guy hadn't spazzed on me for not paying. Big fucking deal!"

"It's a big deal now, isn't it?" Michael shouted back.

"Don't blame me. Blame your retard brother and his freak-out. I tried to stop him, but he beat the living shit out of the guy. What was I supposed to do? He kept shouting 'home' but wouldn't get in my truck. I had to leave him there."

Chris was quickly putting the pieces together. Something didn't add up, and he knew what that something was. "Do you believe that story, Michael?"

"You stay the fuck out of this," Calvin warned, waving the gun at him.

"What are you talking about?" Michael gave Chris a baffled look.

Chris moved his bound hands to his face to wipe away the rain. "The police took samples of the blood at the scene and sent them to the lab. The results came back, and it wasn't Marvin's blood on the victim." He looked directly at Calvin. "Now we know whose blood it is."

"You're full of shit," Calvin shot back, but the cockiness was gone.

"Am I? Marvin gave me the licence number for your Expedition. The cops are running it as we speak. It's only a matter of time before they link that, and then you, to the crime scene. You made the mistake of underestimating Marvin, thinking he was stupid. But he's the reason you're gonna go down."

Chris looked at Michael. "Marvin's going to be cleared. No thanks to your buddy here."

"You lied to me!" Michael raged at Calvin. He reached into his jacket pocket, pulled out a revolver, and pointed it at Calvin. "You were gonna let Marvin rot in jail for something *you* did!"

"What are you gonna do? Shoot *me*? Fuck! Okay, okay. Marvin didn't kill him. I did. But the guy didn't give me a choice. He called me a punk and took a swing at me with his tire iron." He looked at Michael and struck a more conciliatory tone. "I did what I had to do, but me and you can still come out of this on top. Don't you want that?"

He suddenly aimed his gun at Chris.

A shot rang out. A body fell to the ground. Calvin's body. Blood began gushing from his chest.

Chris stared in horror at Calvin's body lying on the ground twitching.

"That's for Marv," Michael shouted at Calvin's

lifeless body. Then he pointed his gun at Chris. "Were you telling the truth?"

"Yes ... I swear to God." Chris realized he wasn't out of danger yet. "I can tell them it was self-defence. I can tell them he was going to shoot me and you saved my life."

The magnitude of what had just happened sank in, and he started to hyperventilate.

Michael stared at Chris for a long moment, as if he was thinking things through. "Relax," he finally said. "I'm not gonna shoot you." He put the safety on his revolver before placing it back in his jacket pocket. He reached into his pants pocket for a knife, walked up to Chris, and cut the rope binding Chris' hands.

"What *are* you going to do?" Chris asked, flexing his hands. He looked down again at Calvin's body, then quickly looked away to avoid puking.

"Don't know. But I'm not sticking around. Got to get the hell out of here." Michael knelt beside Calvin's body and searched through his pockets until he found the keys for the SUV.

Chris was still shaking. "You saved my life. Thank you. I'll tell the police the truth about what happened."

"Doesn't matter. I need to split while I can."

Chris was still struggling to make sense of what had happened: the crash, the abduction, the killing. But he needed to know something, something important. "Why did you do it? Why didn't you let him shoot me?"

Michael looked at him. "It was my fault for not being there for Marv when Calvin came to my door. If I'd been there, none of this would have happened. I let my brother down." He paused. "And then I got to thinking after my call with you that maybe it wasn't such a bad thing with Marv being with you guys. He's better off with you than with me. Ever since Mom died, he's been trapped inside that house. That's no life for anyone. He deserves more than that. I should have got him help but I didn't want people around the house, prying into my business. So when Calvin said he was going to take you out, I knew I couldn't let it happen. It's a life-for-a-life kind of thing."

"What do you mean?"

"I saved your life. Now you gotta save my brother's." He gave Chris a serious look. "Promise you'll do everything you can for him."

Even in his state of shock, Chris was amazed at how protective Michael was of his brother. He realized he envied their relationship. "I'll do what I can. I promise."

"Tell him Mikey says he'll be going home soon." He looked around the empty parking lot and back at Chris. "You got a phone?"

"Uh, yeah."

"Do me a favour. Give me an hour before calling this in. It'll give me a chance to ... Oh, forget it, do what you gotta do. Just look after my brother." He approached the SUV, jumped in, started the engine with a roar, and sped off.

Chris watched the vehicle disappear from sight. When it was gone, he took a deep breath and slowly exhaled.

He looked down at Calvin's body, but this time, he couldn't avoid puking. Now his body was trembling violently from both his ordeal and the rain that had soaked through his clothes.

He reached into his pocket for his cellphone, hesitated for a moment to catch his breath and decide what he was going to say, then dialled 911. He told the operator what had happened and where he was. When the operator ended the call, Chris placed another. Brandon picked up, and Chris filled him in on the details.

"Damn! Are you all right, Chris?"

"Better than Calvin," Chris replied, his voice quavering.

He soon saw the flashing lights of emergency vehicles coming into view through the fog. "The police are on their way. I should go." He decided against calling Stephanie, realizing he'd be in a better position to talk once his shock had lessened.

A convoy of vehicles converged on the scene. The parking lot lit up, the spotlights from police vehicles and ambulances crisscrossing and illuminating the night sky. The lot was being cordoned off with POLICE LINE DO NOT CROSS tape. Chris was bundled onto a gurney and hoisted into an ambulance where paramedics took his vitals and assessed his injuries. A police officer stood by waiting to ask questions about the events leading to the shooting. Chris told him what happened, including Calvin's confession to killing Alberto Bianchi, and Marvin's innocence. A black tarp was prepared for Calvin's body.

It didn't take long for a media van to arrive. A reporter angled her way past the police line trying to get to Chris while her partner shot images of the scene. Chris was reminded somewhat unpleasantly of the last time he'd been inundated by the media at this park, right after he'd rescued Elizabeth Carrier. Unfortunately, Sergeant Ryan wasn't here tonight to shield him from the questions.

"Can you tell us about the body?"

"Did you shoot him?"

"Will you please give the man some breathing room? Can't you see he's been through enough?" Phillip Bernum smiled widely for the reporter while pretending to be outraged. The media crew parted for him. "Good evening, Mr. Ryder. Bit of a press orgy, wouldn't you say?" Bernum laughed, unfazed by the spectacle.

"What are you doing here?"

"I could ask you the same question," the lawyer said through a saccharine smile. "It's a rather interesting story, actually. I happened to be in the area when I heard on my scanner that there was a police incident unfolding at Woodland Park. I thought I'd see if there was anything I could do to help. Quite the coincidence that I'd end up meeting you here, wouldn't you say?"

Coincidence, my ass, Chris thought.

"I see that you're confused, Mr. Ryder. My apologies. I admit it's a bit awkward, our meeting here this evening, given that I'm representing Mr. Owens. By the way, I heard about your recent visit with my client. Tsk, tsk, sir." He waved his index finger. "But don't worry, I'm not going to make a big deal about your indiscretion. I understand how stress can make people act in desperate and irrational ways."

He extended his hand, and again Chris ignored it. "Very well." Bernum's smile faded in mock disappointment.

Then he smiled again. "I hope the remainder of your evening is less eventful" were his parting words as he walked back toward the media crew.

Chris was confused by Bernum's presence. Was it simple coincidence or something more? He was so done in by all that had transpired in the past few hours that he didn't have the energy to give it further thought. He just wanted to sleep.

A paramedic said they were taking Chris to the Health Sciences Centre to be assessed. The door closed, and the vehicle's emergency lights flashed and its siren wailed as it headed off to the hospital.

Chris wasn't keen to be going to the hospital, but the ambulance attendant's small talk provided a good distraction. It must have been an uncharacteristically slow night because he didn't have long to wait before he was whisked through the triage centre and assessed by a physician, who barraged him with questions.

Chris did his best to remain alert, but eventually exhaustion overcame him and he fell into a deep sleep.

THIRTY-EIGHT

Chris awoke completely disoriented. *Where am I? Oh yes, a hospital bed.*

He reached for the call bell beside him, grimacing as pain shot up and down his neck, but he ignored his discomfort because he needed to call Stephanie. He figured she'd be worried because she hadn't heard from him. He pushed the button and a nurse was quick to arrive, offering assistance.

"I need to call someone, let her know where I am."

The nurse smiled. "She's in the waiting room. I'll let her in."

Chris let out a sigh of relief. He was looking forward to finally seeing a familiar face. The door opened, and Deanna walked in.

Her expression told Chris that she had seen the

perplexed look on his face. "They called me. They still have me listed as your next of kin." She smiled as she walked closer to the bed. "How are you feeling?"

"Like I was hit by a truck." He hadn't intended the pun, and it brought a smile to both their faces. He looked at the clock on the wall: seven forty-five. "Is it morning or evening?"

"Morning. You were brought in late last night."

"How long have you been here?"

"A couple hours." She suppressed a yawn.

"I'm sorry, Dee. You didn't need to do this."

"I was worried about you." Before he had a chance to ask the question, she said, "Ann Marie is home. My mother is looking after her."

"She doesn't know?"

Deanna shook her head. "She was already in bed. We both were when the hospital called. I didn't want to wake her, but I wanted to see you."

"Thanks."

"What happened?" she asked in a worried voice. "The hospital said you were in a car accident. But the news I heard on the radio on the way in here said you were at Woodland Park. And a body was found there. Is that true?"

He sighed and touched his head. There was bandage gauze on his forehead. "It's a long story."

"Does it have anything to do with Ray Owens?"

"Good question." He shrugged, wincing as he gingerly moved his shoulder. "The incident had to do with one of my patients. I'm sure Ray is involved somehow." He tried to adjust to a more comfortable position, but the movement hurt his neck.

"Is there anything I can get you? Do you want the nurse?"

"Nah, that's all right. I'll ask for some ibuprofen in a while. I should probably call Stephanie, though."

"Sorry, I didn't have her number or I'd have called her."

"I appreciate you being here, Dee. I really do."

A physician entered the room and told Chris he was lucky to walk away with only moderate symptoms of a soft tissue injury to his neck and shoulder. Chris should expect soreness, swelling, and bruising; treatment options included rest, ice, compression, and elevation. The physician then told him he was ready for discharge, and Chris was advised to check back with his family doctor in a few days, sooner if the symptoms became unmanageable at home.

Deanna offered Chris a ride back to his apartment.

Despite his throbbing neck, the ride home with Deanna was pleasant. The day was promising to be warm and sunny. They talked mostly about their daughter, and Chris agreed with Deanna's suggestion that they reschedule his visit with Ann Marie to a day when he was feeling better.

Finally, they pulled up in front of Chris' apartment building. Chris thanked Deanna again for all that she had done and was about to open the door to step out.

"Ann Marie keeps talking about the aquarium. She wants the three of us to go back." Deanna paused and smiled before continuing. "I'd like that, too."

"That, uh ... would be nice," Chris responded, albeit awkwardly. There it was again, this feeling he had that Deanna wanted to give their relationship another try. Was he right? Or was he reading too much into this?

He had to know, so he blurted out, "What about Walter?"

"I've stopped seeing him."

"Oh, I'm sorry, Dee."

"There's nothing to be sorry about. We ended things okay. He's a nice guy. It's just ... he's not you."

"So what are you saying? You want to give us another shot now? I would have loved that nine months ago, Dee. Believe me, there's nothing in this world I wanted more. But you closed that door firmly. I had no choice but to move on. And as hard as it was, I did. I have moved on, at least I'm trying ... with Stephanie."

Deanna said nothing but tears were forming in her eyes.

"I feel like a jerk, Dee. The last thing I want to do is hurt you. I'll always love you. Nothing's going to change that."

"So I guess that's a no on the aquarium," Deanna said, wiping her eyes. "I should get going. Got to pick up Ann Marie."

"I'll always be there for you, and for Ann Marie," Chris said, stepping out of the car. "You know I will."

"I do."

Chris watched as she drove off, and then entered his building, agonizing over an ever-increasing headache.

Chris checked his phone and saw he had missed calls from Stephanie. He scrolled through the *Tribune* and wasn't surprised to find the headline *Another Body Found at Woodland Park* glaring back at him. Below the headline was a photograph of emergency vehicles in the park's parking lot, cordoned off with police tape. Chris stood there and read the full article, which said the victim's identity was being withheld pending notification of next of kin.

It was when the story mentioned him by name that his pulse rate accelerated and he could feel the familiar tightness in his chest.

Chris Ryder was rushed by ambulance to the Health Sciences Centre with undisclosed injuries. Authorities declined to comment on any connection between Ryder and the body found at the park. Ryder was credited three months ago with rescuing Elizabeth Carrier at Woodland Park, along with discovering the body of Carrier's father, James. Ray Owens was charged with the murder of James Carrier and remains in custody at this time.

He hoped to connect with Stephanie before she found out what happened from the news rather than from him. He called her number.

He was too late. Stephanie had heard the news on the radio when she woke up and was understandably rattled by the time Chris reached her.

"I left you a message last night before I went to bed. I figured you were asleep. Then I wake up this morning and —"

"I'm sorry, Stephanie. I just got home."

"Are you all right?" she asked frantically. "What happened?"

Chris spent the next twenty minutes attempting to reassure Stephanie that he was in fact all right. He skimmed through the events of the previous evening to avoid Stephanie worrying even more about him, and because he wasn't sure how much he should divulge when the police were still investigating.

Despite both his aching body and Stephanie telling him to stay home to rest, Chris decided to go in to work. He knew he was being far too curious for his own good, but he badly needed to find out what would happen with the murder charge against Marvin, now that he himself had helped uncover the identity of the real killer. He gobbled down two ibuprofens and headed for the shower.

THIRTY-NINE

Ray swaggered into the interview room where his visitor was waiting. "Let's get this over with, Bernum. What do you want?"

"Yes, I imagine your social calendar is crammed with constructive tasks and activities," Bernum shot back. He gestured at the stack of newspaper clippings Ray had set down in front of him. "Looks like you've come armed today."

"There's not one story on me that doesn't mention Ryder on the same page."

"Ah, yes, I've had the good fortune of meeting Mr. Ryder. A very determined soul, I must say. He has an uncanny will for survival. They say he's a hero."

"What the fuck makes *him* a hero?"

"Well, consider the facts. You're charged with

killing James Carrier while Mr. Ryder rescued Carrier's daughter. People tend to respond more favourably to rescuers than to killers. They're funny that way," Bernum said, his voice dripping with sarcasm. "But I would think you've got bigger problems than competing with Mr. Ryder for media coverage, wouldn't you?"

"Whose side are you on here?" Ray snapped.

"You know the answer to that, Mr. Owens. Now let's get down to business, shall we? I have some rather unfortunate news for you, with regards to your NCR defence."

"What? Criminally nuts? What's wrong with that?"

"The legal term is *not criminally responsible on account of a mental disorder.*"

"That's the one."

"As your counsel, I'd strongly encourage you to consider alternative options."

"Why can't I claim temporary insanity?"

"I don't see that as a viable option, Mr. Owens. Dr. Stevenson already assessed you, and her recommendation didn't support a finding of not criminally responsible."

"So get another psychiatrist!"

"Believe me, I've exhausted doctor shopping. The fact of the matter is Dr. Stevenson is well regarded in the psychiatric community and from what I've been told her assessment of you was comprehensive. As a result, I haven't been able to find anyone willing to conduct another one." Bernum paused before continuing. "I'm afraid you're going to have to face the fact there's a high probability you'll be found responsible for your actions."

Ray leaned forward in his chair, shortening the distance between him and the lawyer. "Responsible for my actions? That's the best you can come up with? What a joke," he snickered, shaking his head.

"I'm afraid the bad news doesn't end there, Mr. Owens."

"What the hell are you talking about now?"

"Well, for starters, the Crown has considerable evidence against you in the Carrier murder, not the least of which is the fact they have Mr. Ryder as a witness whose evidence will be that you confessed to him in killing Carrier. And then there's the matter of your charge of attempted murder against Mr. Ryder himself."

"So what? That's what you're for."

"So, I think the time has come for you to accept the reality of a considerable period of incarceration."

"What happened to that bullshit line you fed me about having a client interested in taking Ryder out and getting me off the charges?"

"I don't recall being quite that explicit, but nonetheless, Mr. Ryder is no longer a primary interest for my client."

"Why not? He found Carrier's body, and my cellphone. Who knows what else he knows?" Ray said incredulously.

"As a matter of fact, I know exactly what Mr. Ryder knows and what he doesn't know. As your counsel, I've had access to the Court documents including the statement Mr. Ryder provided to the police, which frankly contains nothing of an incriminating nature involving my client's interests."

"So you let him off the hook, just like that?" Ray said with disgust.

"I've also viewed the transcripts from your phone," he said, ignoring Ray's comment. "Again, there's nothing incriminating about my client."

"I could have told you that!"

"And I, of course, would have believed everything coming out of your mouth," Bernum said with a sarcastic smile. "On the other hand, the phone represents a rather bigger problem for you, my friend."

Ray remained silent, as if processing the news. After a long pause he responded. "I know what's going on here. You wanted to be my lawyer to find out how much I knew about the hit on Carrier, and how much dirt those pigs had on me. And now that your so-called client thinks I'm no threat to them, you all throw me under the bus. You're a real slick fucker, aren't you?"

"That's a colourful way of putting it, but generally speaking, your assessment is accurate, Mr. Owens."

"If you think I'm gonna let you use me, and not get something in return, you're even stupider than you look."

"There's no need for that tone, my friend. I'm still prepared to work on your defence. I can stall and drag the trial out as long as possible. For a fee, of course." He looked at a red-faced Ray. "I can see you're upset now, but when you're feeling better, call my secretary. She'll discuss the payment details with you." Bernum stood up and made his way out of the room.

"You think you're done with me. But I'm sure as hell not done with you!" Ray shouted in anger and desperation.

FORTY

Chris' Ranger had been towed away as evidence in the police investigation, but from the amount of damage it had sustained, he figured it was a write-off anyway. He would have to take a taxi to work for the time being.

His ride pulled into the IFP parking lot, and Chris began walking toward the building's entrance. Lucy Chen approached him, recorder in hand. "Mr. Ryder, would you mind if I asked you a few questions?"

He was startled by her sudden appearance from out of nowhere. "Uh ... I can't ... comment."

"Is it true that somebody tried to kill you last night?"

"No comment."

She had hardly waited for his response to her question before lobbing another. "Was last night's incident related to the Marvin Goodwin case?"

"No comment."

"Is it true that the body found at Woodland Park is that of Mr. Bianchi's killer?"

"I'm not answering your questions," he said in a tired voice.

"Any comment on the speculation that the killer is Marvin's brother? Was he an accomplice with Marvin in the killing of Mr. Bianchi?"

Chris had had enough. "You need to get your facts straight."

She gave him a surprised look before responding. "Then why don't you help me get them straight?"

He looked at her, then stared pointedly at her recorder. She got the message, turned off the recorder, and gave him a puzzled look. "What's your deal? Do you have something against the media? Or is it personal, against me?"

"What are you talking about?"

"I've been trying forever to get you to talk with me. You haven't returned my messages."

"It hasn't stopped you, has it?"

"I'm a crime reporter, which means I report on crime."

"I know all about it. You're just doing your job, performing a public service," he said sarcastically.

"As a matter of fact, it *is* a public service. This city, the entire Lower Mainland, for that matter, is gripped by fear over recent violence. People are scared, Mr. Ryder, but they're also angry and tired of feeling powerless. Look at the take-back-the-streets rally being organized for next week. You of all people should appreciate what I'm talking about. You've been involved in incidents that many members of the general public find important and newsworthy: the murder in Woodland Park three months ago, and now this case with Marvin Goodwin. A lot of people would be interested in what you have to say. But you hide behind your hospital's 'no comment' policy or otherwise avoid speaking with me. Can't you speak for yourself? Don't you have your own thoughts?"

Chris laughed cynically. "Sure I do. I think that piece you did with Ray Owens was garbage. But it doesn't matter what I think or say. You'll still find a way to spin it the way you want, to make it more newsworthy, to sell more papers."

"So that's it. It boils down to your biased view of what I do." She shook her head. "So tell me, then, how have I distorted the truth about the Goodwin case?"

"From the moment he was charged, his story was whittled down to a sensationalist sound bite. It didn't matter if it was accurate or not, it sounded good, so people ran with it. 'Crazy man commits brutal murder.' Do you have any idea how many times that headline has run?"

"Are you saying it's not true?"

"It doesn't matter what I say," he countered in frustration. He tried to organize his thoughts, which he found harder than usual, given his current state of mind. "It's one part of the story, but no one is ever in-terested in covering the other parts. The whole story."

"Try me. What's so important about Marvin's case that I've ignored?"

She turned her recorder on and pointed it toward Chris. He remained silent. "Here's your chance," she prodded. "Nothing? Thought so."

Chris was through with her provocation and ex-ploded in a torrent of words. "What about the fact that when your story ran, he was made out to be some kind of monster? Everyone instantly feared and hated him, instantly concluded that he was guilty, instantly screamed that he should never have been out on the street in the first place. Well, you know what? It's true. He shouldn't have been on the street. He was neglect-ed, never given the help he needed. He fell through the cracks, and no one gave a damn. That is, until he was charged with this crime. And now that the charges against him are going to be dropped, *because he's innocent,* no one will give a damn again about what happens to him.

"But he still needs those supports," he continued. "He still needs residential placement with twenty-four-hour care from trained professionals. But will he get it? Don't bet on it. He's gonna be stuck in there —" he pointed to the hospital building "— for God knows how long. But this isn't the right place for him. He doesn't belong here, but the right place for him costs too much money, the right group home, with the right staff. So he'll be here, taking a bed from someone else who desperately needs to be here. So that person waits in jail, where *he* doesn't belong."

He finally took a breath. "But this is complicated. It's not a simple sound bite, so I don't see you running with this story."

"You will now." She clicked the recorder off.

"Be my guest. I don't care."

"It sounds to me like you do care. You care quite a lot." Her tone softened. "For the record, I'm not proud of my piece on Ray Owens. He managed to manipulate me in our interview." She paused before continuing. "But I'm not the enemy, Chris."

"I guess we'll find out." He walked away from Lucy, feeling his already low energy draining away.

It was obvious that news of what had happened to him the night before at Woodland Park had circulated through the hospital. He felt the now-familiar and still-uncomfortable sensation of eyes following his every move. Reaction from his colleagues ranged from concern for his welfare to questions about the juicy details of his latest adventure.

He was just getting settled in his office when Gerald appeared at his door. "Holy shit! What the hell are you doing here?"

"I'm asking myself the same thing." He told Gerald about his run-in with Lucy in the parking lot.

Gerald whistled. "Lord knows what Florence is gonna do when that crap hits the fan."

Chris wanted to talk about something else—anything else. "What's happening with day leaves?"

"I heard Threader the Shredder is going to reinstate them tomorrow. Word is there were no surprises with the internal review. We have sufficient policies and contingency plans in place for patients going into the community."

"So the protocols were followed when Perry went UA?" Chris asked, although he wasn't surprised that a review would come to that logical conclusion.

Gerald nodded and smiled. "The Ministry's happy with the report and public confidence is restored, so it's a win-win for everyone!"

"I'm not feeling much like a winner right now."

Gerald grew serious. "No, I guess not. I can't imagine what you're feeling right now. But if you want to talk, you know how to reach me, okay?" Chris nodded in agreement. "Well, I'll let you get caught up."

To his great surprise, Chris managed to get some paperwork done before ambling over to Dr. Stevenson's office, where he found her sitting in front of her computer, scrolling through the local CBC website.

"I didn't expect to see you here today. How do you feel?" She stood up to greet him.

He shrugged. "I've been better."

"Are you sure you should be here? Maybe you should be at home resting?"

"I'd just be staring at the walls all day. Besides, I wanted to hear what's going on with Marvin."

She shook her head and smiled. "Of course you do." Leaning over her keyboard, she surfed through the news items. "I had a call this morning from Marvin's lawyer informing me that Crown agrees with her recommendation on having the charges against Marvin dropped. Apparently, though, this information has already been leaked to the media. Marvin's lawyer told me the police will be releasing a statement this morning."

She looked up over her shoulder at Chris. "Is it true about Marvin's brother?"

Chris updated her briefly on what had happened at Woodland Park the night before. Their conversation was interrupted by a BREAKING NEWS headline running at the top of the computer screen.

"This must be it." She clicked on the caption and they huddled in front of the monitor to read the statement.

> Members of the RCMP responded to a 911 call last night at Woodland Park. When officers arrived, they discovered a body at the scene. The Major Crimes Unit has now taken over this file. The identity of the deceased will not be released until next of kin have been notified.

The statement went on to say that Crown was considering a stay of proceedings in the charges against Marvin Goodwin and that Michael Goodwin was considered a person of interest. Police were appealing to him to contact his local police detachment. The statement also indicated that police were not yet in a position to comment on Chris Ryder's presence at Woodland Park, other than to clarify that he had cooperated with the investigation and was not considered a person of interest.

Dr. Stevenson closed the site. "Well, it's good to hear you're cooperating with the investigation," she said lightheartedly to Chris. "I'm surprised you haven't been pursued for an interview."

"Actually ..." Chris told her about his encounter with Lucy Chen. "It wasn't one of my brighter moments. I have no idea how it's going to turn out."

"Let's take a look." Dr. Stevenson logged on to the *Tribune*'s website and scrolled down until she saw a piece by Lucy Chen reporting on the discovery of the body at Woodland Park the night before.

Chris felt a moment of panic.

They skimmed through the article in silence. Lucy started by saying that the previous evening's incident at Woodland Park was believed to be related to the Marvin Goodwin case involving the brutal murder of ice cream vendor Alberto Bianchi. She outlined how Marvin Goodwin had initially been charged in connection with that murder.

They then saw that Lucy Chen had filed a secondary story, headlined *Marvin Goodwin: From Suspect to Victim*. Parts of the story were drawn from Chris' outburst.

> Mr. Goodwin is a young man with complex medical needs, which include severe symptoms of

autistic spectrum disorder and intellectual disability. As a result, he experiences significant communication and functioning challenges. It appears that these challenges make Mr. Goodwin an easy target in taking the fall for Mr. Bianchi's murder.

While the identity of the killer is unknown at this time, what is clear is that it is not Mr. Goodwin. He will receive a stay of proceedings in this criminal matter.

Despite that development, Mr. Goodwin is likely to remain hospitalized at IFP due to a lack of services to meet his special care needs in the community.

Lucy had quoted liberally from her interview with Chris on how Marvin had been "neglected" and "fell through the cracks." But the article finished with an unexpected turn:

Mr. Goodwin is a prime example of the human cost of cutbacks in funding for clients of Community Living Society, cutbacks that have been directed by the provincial government.

Starting next week, the *Vancouver Tribune* will be examining these issues in depth, including the role the provincial Ministry of Health has played by clawing back services to this vulnerable population over the last three years.

Chris' ears were burning as he read the quotes attributed to him. They were accurate renditions of what he had said, but he knew he was going to catch hell from his director for sharing his insights with the media. Still, he'd underestimated Lucy Chen's integrity. He made a mental note to apologize to her.

Dr. Stevenson must have read his mind. "Ouch, this is not going to go over well with Florence."

"Don't suppose it will."

"But I have to give Lucy credit. She's done a good job of highlighting the challenges we're going to have in getting Marvin out of here."

FORTY-ONE

It would only be a matter of time, Chris knew, before he'd be summoned to Florence's office to account for his actions.

He realized that he'd made a serious mistake in coming to work today. The events of the last several days had rendered him unprepared to deal with even the daily rigours of his job, let alone the intense pressure he was feeling from the Goodwin case. He was a wreck.

His office phone rang. He figured this was Florence calling and thought of letting the call go to voicemail, but he picked up, realizing there was no point in stalling the inevitable.

"Ryder! How the hell are ya?"

Talking to Ray was the last thing Chris needed right now. His heart pounded and he felt nauseated.

But like a moth drawn to a flame, he couldn't resist. "What do you want, Ray?"

"Just checking up on my dear little brother. Heard about your accident at our favourite haunting ground. Haven't I always said you're not out of the woods yet?" He guffawed.

Chris was in no mood now for Ray's games and was seriously considering hanging up.

"I hear you met my lawyer, too. He's gonna get me out of here. Gonna find me criminally nuts."

"You're bluffing, Ray. I know all about your lawyer's failed attempts at getting a psychiatrist to do an NCR assessment. Meanwhile, the bodies are starting to pile up. Carrier, Goode—and they're just the ones we know about. If I were you, I'd be worried about your past coming back to haunt you."

"What are you talking about, Ryder?"

"I'm talking about your foster sister."

"What about her?"

"I hear Teresa died from a drug overdose a few years back."

"So what?"

"The police found bruises on her wrist. They didn't think she was alone at the time of her death."

"What does this have to do with me?" Ray sounded rattled.

"Who knows? But I wonder what they'd find if they reopened the case and looked at the file with fresh eyes, maybe checking to see whether prints had been taken at the scene, checked for DNA. Little things like that. It's amazing what technology can do today. But you already know that, considering what they could find on your cellphone. I'll be interested to see what they come back with when they dig into Teresa's case."

"Move on, Ryder. You're stuck in the past."

"Pot calling the kettle black, Ray? You blame me for all your problems. You're the one who can't let go of the past."

Silence on the line. Chris waited. He knew Ray would have a comeback. "Well, I guess that's another tie that binds us, brother dear. And by the time I'm done, you'll be just like me. Alone. Our old man is off my 'kick the bucket' list. Guess who's next?"

Chris didn't have the strength to fight anymore. He knew what he wanted to say to Ray, and what he wanted to do to him. But he stopped himself. He'd acted impulsively enough for one day. It was time for a different approach. "It doesn't have to be that way, Ray."

"Of course it does. Why would I want it any other way?" Ray sneered.

"Because you have a son."

"What?"

"So you didn't know?"

"What the hell are you talking about?"

Chris thought Ray sounded genuinely surprised. He picked up something else in Ray's response that he hadn't observed before: vulnerability. "I don't know the details, but yeah, you've got a son. He's in the care of the Ministry. The same Ministry you blame for what happened to you. I know about the abuse, Ray: the bedwetting, the strapping, the bullying. What happened to you was wrong. And I know you felt abandoned."

"Why are you telling me this, Ryder? You think I'm suddenly gonna turn over a new leaf just 'cause I got a runt running around? Life ain't that simple."

"I'm not saying it is. It's hard, and sometimes it's not fair. But you have the chance to play some kind of role in your son's life. It could be a positive one, *if* you tried doing something good with your own life. Starting now."

"Even if I *do* have a kid, there's nothing I can do about it now. There's no way they're gonna let me see him. They're not gonna think I can change, and you don't, either. Would you trust me with your daughter?"

Chris said nothing.

"Didn't think so. I'm not going to change, Ryder. But at least I'm not a hypocrite like you. You talk this shit about the power of change, but when it comes right down to it, you don't believe it."

"I believe you can try."

"I'll tell you what I believe, Ryder. You're no different than me, no better than me, and I'm gonna prove it."

"There's nothing for you to prove, Ray. I already know where we're alike. We both had shitty childhoods. I lost my mother, and you were abused in foster care. It's left a mark on both of our lives."

"Boo-hoo. Give me a break, Ryder."

Chris ignored him. "But that's where the similarity ends. You wanna stay stuck, and mad at the world forever, that's your decision. But I don't want to be like you, and I'm going to make sure that never happens. That includes these games. I'm tired of them. You're taking up too much space in my head and you're not worth it."

"You think this is a game, Ryder. Wrong! This is the real deal, and you'd better look over your shoulder, little brother, 'cause before you know it, I'll be back at your shithole IFP making every day of your pathetic little life a living hell. It's what I dream about!"

"Well, dream on, Ray. We both know you're never going to be found NCR. And we both know you're never coming back to IFP." He stopped to let his point sink in before delivering his final blow. "And we both know you're going to be spending a *long* time in jail. You were right about one thing though. I've been stuck in the past. It's time to move on and leave you behind."

"Your days are numbered, Ryder. You're my next victim."

Chris paused for a long moment. "Well, I'm not gonna waste any more of them on you. And I'll tell you something else. I'm nobody's victim."

He hung up. He'd never have thought that ending a phone call could be so gratifying and bring so much closure. But this wasn't any old phone call: this was Ray Owens. And for the first time in several months Chris felt a weight lift off his shoulders. He was finally ready to leave Ray behind.

"Please tell me the Ray you were just talking to was *not* Ray Owens."

Chris sat up with a start. It was Florence. How long had she been there? And how much had she heard?

"Uh ... hi, Florence." He felt his cheeks burning red hot.

Florence entered the office and closed Chris' door with some force. "Why were you talking to Ray Owens?" She remained standing, looking down at a seated Chris and shaking her head.

"I didn't know it was him when he called."

"Why was he calling you in the first place?"

Chris gave a nervous laugh. "Why does he do any of the things he does? He was looking to get a reaction."

The long, hard look she gave him felt like she was running her personal lie detector test. He must have passed because she took a seat and broke the silence.

"That can't be easy," she said in a way that to Chris' mind actually bordered on empathy. "I caught the last part of your conversation, in case you were wondering. The man is a royal pain in the ass. He revels in his ability to terrorize. I really hope you're able to put him behind you."

"Thank you." He was shocked by her support.

Florence shifted in her chair, the expression on her face becoming stern. "I came to see you about the interview you gave Lucy Chen." The hardness had returned to her voice.

"I screwed up, I know."

"Why? That's what I don't understand. You could have kept walking, kept your mouth shut. Why did you talk with her? Can you help me understand that?"

"Lucy caught me at a really bad time. She was talking about Marvin, about Woodland Park. She didn't have all the facts. But I acted without thinking." He was slow to look her in the eye, wary of her response.

Florence didn't respond immediately. She seemed to be deliberating.

Chris knew he'd used up all of his get-out-of-jail-free cards with her. He knew she'd be within her rights to suspend him, perhaps even to fire him now. She was pissed at what he had done. Hell, he was pissed at himself.

"I explicitly told you not to talk with the media. Our communications department is much better equipped to respond in a professional and dispassionate manner to media questions on sensitive matters. What you did was the exact opposite. You allowed the reporter's questions to get to you. You took it personally. You spoke from your heart, not your head."

"I know —"

"Let me finish!" She took a deep breath and slowly

let it out. "What you did was careless, and it's causing me a lot of grief. This case was already high profile, and your outburst has taken it to a whole new level. I just got off the phone with the health minister. She's been put in the position of having to defend the Ministry's actions in terms of the Community Living Society. I'm told they'll be giving a press conference in the coming days to defend their cutbacks to services. No doubt they'll deflect their responsibility and place it squarely at the feet of CLS."

She looked at Chris and exposed a flicker of a smile. "There is, however, an upside to the situation. Your interview and the *Tribune*'s pending series of stories have put pressure on the Ministry to respond to the lack of services for clients like Marvin. They want to save face, and they intend to use Marvin to do it."

"How?"

"By announcing that he's been accepted for placement in a twenty-four-hour licensed care home."

"Really?" Chris was flabbergasted.

"It's their way of showing there's no problem with the system. Coming up with a bed for Marvin demonstrates that the wait-lists are not as bad as have been reported. And," she added, a cynical tone creeping into her voice, "the Ministry comes out smelling like roses."

"Do you know where the home will be?"

"No. I guess we'll find that out at the dog-and-pony show. And I'm willing to bet they'll all be on site for the photo-op when Marvin is admitted to his new home."

She paused for a moment before continuing. "My point in coming to see you was to let you know that your interview with Lucy Chen helped Marvin in a way that I couldn't. We both know IFP isn't the right place for him." She paused again before adding. "I also wanted to give you fair warning that the Ministry has you in their crosshairs now. The minister was not impressed with your interview and its repercussions for them. There's considerable pressure on me, as your director, to make sure you don't step out of line again. I thought you should know."

"Thanks, Florence."

"So consider yourself warned. The next time you disregard my orders, I will personally deliver your walking papers."

"It won't happen again."

"Good." She looked him over. "Now go home. You look terrible."

Chris breathed a sigh of relief when she left, content that he still had his job. He loved working with his patients and their families, and he enjoyed the camaraderie with his colleagues.

He agreed with Florence, though: recent events had caught up with him. It seemed everyone around him was echoing her concern; the question was what he would do about it. Right now, all he knew was that he had a few details to sort through, and then he'd be on his way home. The thought of seeing Stephanie later that evening lifted him out of his melancholy mood.

He looked at his watch. It was time for his meeting with Dr. Stevenson. He made his way to Alpha Unit, where he endured some light-hearted ribbing from the nursing staff about his latest exploits. Even Alex showed him no mercy. "Just finished reading the latest in the Chronicles of Ryder. What do you do for an encore?" he said to gales of laughter from the other staff.

Dr. Stevenson arrived and bailed Chris out by leading him and Alex to a meeting room. Alex updated them on Marvin, and Chris shared the highlights of his conversation with Florence. Alex left the room to get Marvin and returned a short while later with the young man, clutching his copy of the Vancouver Canucks program.

Marvin sat down warily and uttered his now-familiar word: "Home." He shyly looked at the faces of the three other people in the room, finally resting his gaze on Chris.

"We were just talking about that," Chris said. "We've got some good news. We've found a home for you."

He stopped to let the news register with Marvin. The young man looked away from them and then down at the program. He didn't seem fazed by the announcement.

"Would you be interested in seeing the house

in a little while?" Still no response, but Chris gently pressed on. "You could bring your program with you, if you like. In fact, you could even decorate your home with Canucks posters, any way you like. It's your home."

Marvin looked up from his program, directly at Chris, and showed more than a hint of a smile. "Home."

"Yeah, Marvin. Home."

FORTY-TWO

A thought stopped Chris on his way back to his office, redirecting him to his manager's office. He wasn't sure what he was going to say. He wasn't even sure if David would be there. But he felt he'd put off the inevitable long enough.

He arrived to find David sitting at his desk reviewing a report. "Have you got a minute?" Chris asked apprehensively as he stood in the doorway.

David put the paper down. "I've been looking for you. Close the door, please." Chris did as he was told and remained standing. "About that interview ..." he said, giving Chris a surprised look.

"Yeah, I know. That's why I'm here. I'm not sure ... This isn't easy for me." He breathed in and slowly let the air out. Then in a rush he said, "I think I need to take some time off work." Saying the words out loud startled him. But Chris also felt immense relief.

David gave him a sympathetic look. "Whatever time you need, Chris, I'll support you."

"I've been putting this off for ... for who knows how long. I should have taken time off after Ray Owens and Woodland Park. I dunno, maybe I didn't want to admit I had a problem. And I guess I thought if I was busy, it would distract me. But it hasn't worked out that way. It's taken a long time for me to realize that I was in denial about how bad things had gotten." He thought back to his foolhardy trips to unknown houses, his irresponsible behaviour at his daughter's dance studio, his interview with Lucy. "I need to make some changes."

He looked away from his manager, his eyes settling on a snow globe on a shelf next to him. He picked it up and shook it. "My life feels a lot like this. It's been shaken up and I don't know what's what anymore. I need to take some time to figure out what to do, get things under control." Chris gently placed the ornament back on its shelf.

"I think you're doing the right thing, Chris. Whatever time you need to take, you'll have my full support. Your job will be here when you're ready to come back."

"Social Work 101, right? I have to help myself before being able to help someone else." Chris shook his head at the cliché.

"It's true. You're good at helping your patients, but who helps you?"

"It's kinda hard for me talk about. But I know I have to do it."

"You call me when you're ready to come back, and don't worry about anything else. We'll work it out, okay?"

"Yeah, thanks, David." He opened the door and left, feeling awkward and embarrassed but also relieved.

Back in his office, Chris responded to a few patient-related matters and packed up his belongings.

He knew he didn't have it in him to go anywhere or do anything that evening, so he placed a call to Stephanie, who offered to spend the night at his place, and he quickly accepted. He ordered a taxi home.

As his ride drove away from the IFP parking lot, he looked back as the building slowly receded in the distance.

He didn't know when he'd be returning to the place that for the last ten years had been a second home to him. He felt a quiet sadness passing over him but knew in his heart that he was doing the right thing.

FORTY-THREE

When Chris arrived home, he called Nathaniel and upon receiving his voicemail, left a message to schedule their next meeting. He knew he had his work cut out for him with his future counselling sessions, but for the first time he felt optimistic about that future.

Chris grabbed a gel ice pack from his freezer and wrapped it around his neck to lessen the aching. He hit the Play button on his iPod and flopped down on the futon, content to shut his eyes and take a well-needed rest.

The ringing of his phone disturbed his peace. It was Brandon Ryan. "You gonna be there awhile?"

"Yeah. Stephanie's coming over later, but you're welcome to drop by."

"Okay. I'll bring the beer this time."

Chris lay back as Led Zeppelin filled his apartment. He was listening to Robert Plant sing about a faraway land of ice and snow and letting his thoughts drift when a knock at the door brought him back to reality. He was groggy and slow to respond, a fact not lost on Brandon, who stood there with a pizza and a six-pack.

"Damn, you look like hell!" Brandon walked into the kitchen, opened a bottle of Granville Island Pilsner, and offered it to Chris. "This is your brand, right?"

"Yeah, but I'll pass."

Brandon took a slice of pizza and offered the box to Chris. "Figured you might be running low."

"Thanks," Chris mumbled through a mouthful.

"Read your interview." Chris just grunted. "Caught the news on Marvin, too. Congrats. That kid is lucky he had you in his corner. Good job. And I have some news for you."

"Yeah?" Chris said with wide eyes.

"Michael Goodwin was arrested near the BC–Alberta border about an hour ago. He'd ditched the SUV and stolen a car, but RCMP had already been tracking his movements from the licence plate info you provided—or to be precise, Marvin provided." Brandon filled Chris in on the developments in the case. The SUV had been registered to Calvin Johnson. The first address Chris had sent did in fact belong to Marvin and his brother, the second to Calvin.

"With the blood analysis results, it's only a matter of time before Calvin is officially declared Alberto Bianchi's killer."

Chris felt a shiver go up his spine as his thoughts turned to Calvin, of how he'd nearly been killed by him and then the sight of his dead body. "I'm just glad it's all over."

Brandon nodded in agreement and took a gulp of his beer. "Well, I can see you need some rest. I'll leave you to it." Brandon had his hand on the door handle when he looked back at Chris. "Hey, you really did good with Marvin."

Stephanie greeted Brandon as he stepped out of the elevator on the ground floor of Chris' building. They exchanged hugs. "How's he doing?"

"He seems all right to me, considering the circumstances," Brandon replied, then added with a smile, "which is more than I can say for his apartment. How *do* you put up with it?"

"We all have our crosses to bear." She rolled her eyes and motioned to the plant she was carrying. "I bought him this. I hope he doesn't kill it."

"You're a brave woman."

"At least he's got us to keep him on the straight and narrow," she said lightly. "Keep him out of trouble, okay?" She stepped inside the elevator.

"I'll do my best." As the door started to close, Brandon added, "He's doing all right for himself."

FORTY-FOUR

Chris held the door for Stephanie and welcomed her inside his apartment.

She placed the plant on his kitchen counter and threw her arms around him, kissing him softly.

"I should get attacked more often. You even come bearing gifts!"

"Don't even joke about that! Where does it hurt?"

"I've got a killer headache. I'm waiting for the ibuprofen to kick in. Got some bad news, though." He paused. "My truck didn't make it."

She shook her head, not the slightest bit amused. "Why aren't you taking this more seriously?"

"Okay." He put his hands up in mock surrender. "But maybe you can help me pick out a new truck once the insurance is cleared."

"I don't really care about that right now. A car can be replaced anytime. What did the hospital say?"

"Bad case of whiplash. If the symptoms get worse, I need to see my doctor. Oh, and I need *a lot* of TLC."

"And your only symptom is headaches?" she asked, ignoring his last wisecrack. "Not your *only* symptom, you know what I mean," she corrected herself.

"I'm fine, Stephanie. Really."

"I read your interview with the *Tribune*."

She looked at him closely, and Chris knew she was observing his reaction. He sighed and struggled to come up with a rational explanation but found none.

"I've made mistakes. That was one of them."

"How much trouble did you get into?"

He shrugged. "Could have been worse. It was a wake-up call, made me realize I need to make some changes."

"What kind of changes?"

"I shouldn't have gone back to work so fast. I should have listened to you. All I can say is, I'm listening now." He paused. "I'm taking a medical leave of absence. I'm ready to commit fully to counselling. I know I need it. I left a message for Nathaniel." Now it was Chris who was looking for a reaction.

"Starting when?"

"Now."

"I ... I don't know what to say. I know how hard that must have been for you. But I think it's the right decision."

"Yeah," he said wistfully. He walked into the kitchen, craving a rum and cola but settling on a glass of water. He moved into the living room and plopped himself onto his futon. Stephanie joined him. "By the way, Brandon was here."

"I know. I ran into him on the way in." They were silent for a moment before Chris continued.

"The other mistake I made was turning away from you when I needed you most. At the time, I couldn't help but feel you were seeing me at my worst. And that's not the real me. That's why I didn't want to talk with you about it, because I didn't want to weigh you down with my problems. But I realize now that I have to be more open with you. And I will. And I'm going to do everything I possibly can to get better and make *us* work."

"I know the last three months have been hell for you, Chris. But that hasn't changed the way I feel about you. And what's that saying 'for better or worse'?" she said with a smile.

"It will be for better, I make that promise to you. I've also been thinking about us living together." The look she gave him combined eagerness and surprise. "I know the timing isn't the best with everything that's happened. But that's also why it's so important. I don't ever want to lose you."

"You're not going to lose me. I'm not going anywhere."

Chris drew her into his arms. "I'm so lucky to have

you in my life. When my mind went to dark places, all I saw before was Ray, and I'd feel powerless and hopeless. But now when I'm low, I think of you and I feel hope. That's what you are to me, Stephanie, you're my hope. I love you."

"I love you too, Chris," she said, swiping at her wet eyes.

"I want us to start a new life together. I want to hold you tight, every night. And wake up with you by my side, every morning. I want us to get a new place. We'll make it *our* place. Our home. You. Me. Our family."

AUTHOR'S AFTERWORD

This story, although fictional, was inspired by my experiences working in a forensic psychiatric hospital for over twenty years. While my primary goal was to entertain, there were a few things on my mind as I was writing this story. One was the stigma towards "forensic" patients; another was the stress that caregivers often experience when providing care; and another was a general point on how mental health issues are perceived in comparison to physical health issues.

Over the course of working in a forensic psychiatric hospital I've witnessed friction between criminal justice and mental health; it plays out in the public debate in our communities on issues such as who is in need of mental health care and who is in need of incarceration. Unfortunately, when we approach these issues with a closed mind, the debate contributes to the stigmatization of individuals involved with forensic psychiatric services. I've also witnessed the effects of vicarious trauma that those in the helping professions (nursing, social work, psychology, psychiatry, etc.) may experience when they work with the victims of trauma.

There's a degree of stigma associated with having a mental health challenge independent of any involvement with the forensic system. Fortunately, there's growing awareness and acceptance towards treating mental health challenges similar to physical health challenges, so we can hope that one day there will be no shame in reaching out for help when one is struggling with anxiety, depression, or other mental health issues, just as there's no shame in reaching out for help when one is struggling with physical health conditions such as diabetes or heart disease. I hope readers perceive both the urgency and the hope running through this novel.

ACKNOWLEDGEMENTS

Writing this book, and the process of getting it published, was truly a labour of love. *Labour*, because it involved sustained hard work, and periods when I experienced highs and lows, along with times when, quite frankly, I questioned what I was doing and why I was doing it. *Love*, because even during those moments of self-doubt I believed there was a story worth telling, if only I could get it right. I hope I got it right. If I did, it's due to the large team of supporters who helped me at various points along the way.

I start with the great team at NeWest Press, including Leslie Vermeer for her outstanding editing, as well as the suggestion for the book title! I thank General Manager Matt Bowes for believing my early manuscript submissions showed promise and for maintaining interest in working with me. I thank Claire Kelly for her amazing work as production manager, helping me turn my dream into reality. Huge thanks also go out to Kate Hargreaves for her design work, Isabel Yang with her marketing expertise, and Christine Kohler for her office administrative wizardry.

My sincere thanks and appreciation go out to Sam Wiebe and A.J. Devlin.

I owe so much to my wonderful family, including my wife, Tanya, and our children, Lauren and Matthew. You mean the world to me, and I thank you for your unwavering support. I've lost count of how many early versions of the story my parents Barb and Alan Carew read, but I remember their encouragement every step of the way. I also want to acknowledge the support of my mother- and father-in-law, Donna and Rob Proctor.

There are several other people I wish to thank, and while I'm sure I haven't captured everyone here (and I apologize for anyone I may have accidentally overlooked), I'd like to acknowledge the following: Eugene Wang; LeeAnne Meldrum; Esko Kajander; Cheryl Freedman and Elaine Freedman; Sylvia Taylor; Jodi Renner; Andrew Pike; Kelly Hart; Bryna Dominguez; Christopher Robertson; Debra Purdy Kong; John Thistle; Lorri Mitchell; Wendy Carew Mayner; Gary Carew; Gary Wilson; Debbie and Robert Rideout; Cynthia Whelan; and Gordon Carew.

D.B. CAREW is a crime fiction writer who was born in Newfoundland and Labrador. He now lives in Coquitlam, British Columbia, with his wife and their two children. Derrick has worked at the provincial forensic psychiatric hospital for more than twenty years, and his experience as a social worker serves as inspiration for his novels. His first book, *The Killer Trail*, was shortlisted in 2013 for the Crime Writers Association (CWA) Debut Dagger for unpublished manuscript and was published by NeWest Press in 2014. His website can be found at www.dbcarew.com.